"Sophia, where are

Hadley pressed past Ryan.

A cool gust of wind blew across the room, sending a chill up Ryan's spine. The emergency escape window showed signs of having been pried open.

"Sophia!" Hadley cried and tried to brush past him again.

"No. You can't go rushing out there, you'll get yourself killed. Stay—" He'd almost said *stay here* but that wouldn't work. The shooter could circle back and get Hadley, too.

"You have to come with me. I can't leave you here unprotected."

"You better believe I'm coming with you."

"Listen." He grasped her upper arms and forced her to look at him. "If you rush out there recklessly, it could get you killed—"

"I don't care. I've got to—"

"Yes, you do. You don't want to leave Sophia without a mother. And if you do anything reckless, you could jeopardize her life, too." She visibly blanched, and he knew his words had had the desired effect. "They can't have gotten far. Let's go."

Ryan prayed he was right, and Sophia would be back in her mother's arms within the hour.

Rhonda Starnes is a retired middle school language arts teacher who dreamed of being a published author from the time she was in seventh grade and wrote her first short story. She lives in North Alabama with her husband, who she lovingly refers to as Mountain Man. They enjoy traveling and spending time with their children and grandchildren. Rhonda writes heart-and-soul suspense with rugged heroes and feisty heroines.

Books by Rhonda Starnes

Love Inspired Suspense

Rocky Mountain Revenge
Perilous Wilderness Escape
Tracked Through the Mountains
Abducted at Christmas

Visit the Author Profile page at LoveInspired.com.

ABDUCTED AT CHRISTMAS

RHONDA STARNES

LOVE INSPIRED SUSPENSE
INSPIRATIONAL ROMANCE

LOVE INSPIRED® SUSPENSE
INSPIRATIONAL ROMANCE

ISBN-13: 978-1-335-59914-8

Abducted at Christmas

For questions and comments about the quality of this book, please contact us
at CustomerService@Harlequin.com.

Love Inspired
22 Adelaide St. West, 41st Floor
Toronto, Ontario M5H 4E3, Canada
www.LoveInspired.com

Printed in U.S.A.

For I know the thoughts that I think toward you,
saith the Lord, thoughts of peace, and not of evil,
to give you an expected end.
—*Jeremiah* 29:11

For my dad. The first man I ever loved, and the one who taught me the characteristics of a true hero.

ONE

Hadley Logan pulled into the driveway of her 1920s Craftsman bungalow and released a contented sigh, allowing the stress of the day to fade away. Adorned with white Christmas lights, the beautiful house she'd spent the last two years turning into a home was even more inviting. Her sanctuary. It was the one place that always made her feel safe. And for the next two weeks, she planned to live like a hermit, cocooned inside with her daughter.

As she glanced in the rearview mirror, a smile lifted the corners of her mouth. Five-year-old Sophia had fallen asleep on the ride, her head tilted to one side with her curly strawberry blond hair draped in ringlets across her face.

After a brief internal battle, Hadley decided it would be best to carry all of her bags into the house and then return for Sophia. This way, if her precious daughter woke up while being transferred indoors, all of the groceries and things would already be inside.

She looped the strap of her crossbody purse over her head and then stepped out into the bright sunlight. Closing her eyes, she tilted her face heavenward. *Hello, Christmas break.*

Hadley opened her eyes and watched the cold vapor of her breath drift into the air, carrying with it the weight of the burden of being a single parent with a full-time job as a high school history teacher. For the next fourteen days, she would simply be Sophia's mom. No papers to grade, no parent conferences and no ball games or other extracurricular activities requiring her to work overtime.

She smiled and moved to the back of her car. Thankfully, the sun had melted the remnants of snow off the sidewalk and driveway that had been left behind after the neighbor's teenage son had shoveled for her late yesterday afternoon, though plenty of the cold, white stuff still lingered on the grassy areas. The small snowman she and Sophia had built that stood guard in the middle of the front yard had also partially melted, losing several inches of height and leaning so much to one side that his hat dipped over one of his eyes and one of his twig arms almost touched the ground. Maybe it was a good thing Sophia had fallen asleep—she would be heartbroken when she saw the snowman. Of course, on the morning news, the weatherman had predicted ten inches of snow to fall overnight, so they could build a bigger snowman tomorrow.

Pressing the release button for the trunk, Hadley slipped the handle of the blue canvas bag that held her planner and the teacher edition of the ninth grade US History textbook over her right shoulder. She quickly gathered the six bags of groceries, sliding her left arm through the handles of three of them and her right arm through two, then picked up the heaviest bag with the gallon of milk with her right hand. No sense making multiple trips when she could manage in one. Besides, the faster she unloaded the car, the quicker she could get Sophia inside out of the cold.

It wasn't until she was on the front porch that she realized she'd forgotten to take her keys out of her purse. Owning a vehicle with keyless entry and push-button start was great except for times like this, when she needed to get her keys from her purse and her hands were full. Switching the bag holding the milk to her left hand, she dug into her purse one-handedly. Where was her keychain? There. She almost had it. If she could just get her balance.

Hadley leaned against the door for support, and it swung open. She fell onto the hardwood floor with an *umph*. Dazed, she lay there and wondered why the door was unlatched. Hadn't she secured the house when they left home? She quickly replayed the events of the morning. Sophia, happy and excited about her class Christmas party, had bounced around constantly asking if it were time to go. Once they were in the car, Hadley realized she'd forgotten her phone and had returned to retrieve it. Maybe she hadn't pulled the door closed completely. Oh, well, she couldn't change it now. Hopefully, the eggs hadn't broken in the fall.

After untangling herself from the bags, she used the entryway bench for support to pick herself up off the floor, turned and froze.

Her home had been ransacked. The Christmas tree, coffee table, sofa and a chair had been turned over. Cushions, papers, toys and the laundry Hadley had been too tired to fold last night were strewn about. She took a few steps into the room and gaped.

The open floor plan gave her a clear view of the kitchen where cabinet doors hung open and drawers were dumped on the floor. No, this couldn't be happening. Her heart raced. Had Troy found them?

It had been six years since she ran from her abusive ex-boyfriend after one of his rages had sent her to the ER and she discovered she was pregnant. Knowing if she stayed she would not only put her own life but also that of her unborn child in jeopardy had forced her to disappear. As each year had passed, she'd relaxed more and more, thinking she and her daughter were safe. But they weren't. And now, Troy would know she hadn't had the abortion as he'd demanded.

If it weren't for her unplanned pregnancy, there was no telling how long she would have put up with the abuse. He'd told her he'd kill her if she ever tried to leave him, and she'd believed him. But the need to keep her baby safe had empowered her to put her fear of death aside and flee. In a way, Sophia had saved Hadley's life.

A door slammed at the back of the house where the bedrooms were located. Fear immobilized her, and her body began to shake uncontrollably. Sophia! It was up to her to keep Sophia out of the hands of the monster who was biologically her father.

Pushing the grocery bags out of the way with her feet, she searched for her keys. She had to get her daughter to safety. Frantic, she dropped to her knees, searching under and around the bench. A glint of metal next to the gallon of milk caught her attention. Footsteps pounded in the hallway. She snatched her keys with her left hand and grasped the handle of the milk firmly with her right. The footsteps drew closer. She rose upward and swung with all her might, hitting the intruder on the side of his head with the gallon of milk. A man wearing a black knit cap and a camo neck gaiter pulled over his mouth and nose staggered backward, white liquid dripping down his head.

Hadley spun and raced out of the house, the man right behind her.

A black SUV pulled into the driveway and screeched to a halt. The intruder muttered an oath, pushed her down the steps, leaped off the porch and vanished around the side of the house.

A dark-haired man with black-rimmed glasses got out of the SUV, a gun in his hand, and sprinted to her. "Emma, are you okay?"

The sound of the name she had buried almost six years ago sent a chill—a thousand times colder than the Wyoming winter—up her spine and wrapped around her chest. Her heart constricted and, for a moment, she forgot how to breathe.

"Are you okay?" he asked again.

She nodded, unable to form words as she fought to ward off shock.

"Stay here. Call nine-one-one," the stranger yelled as he took off in the direction the intruder had gone.

Her mind whirled at warped speed. This couldn't be happening. Past mistakes had almost cost her Sophia's life and hers, but with the help of her friend Jessica, who had also experienced Troy's abuse, she had managed to change her identity and escape. And until today, life as Hadley Logan had been better than any life she could have ever imagined. One thing was certain: she would never go back to being Emma Bryant.

Her keys still clutched in her hand, she pushed to her feet and rushed to her vehicle. Thankfully, Sophia was still asleep. She desperately wanted to drive away with her daughter. Only, she couldn't because the dark-haired man had completely blocked her vehicle with his. And attempting to drive across the soggy, snow-covered yard would be futile. Berating herself for not spending the extra money for the all-wheel drive option, she slid behind the steering wheel, locked the doors and started the engine. Then she pulled out her phone and dialed 911, the entire time keeping her eyes on the surrounding area. All-wheel drive or not, if the intruder came back, she'd plow across the yard and get her child to safety.

Ryan Vincent fought through the thick underbrush and briars that bordered the back of Emma's property, coming out on the other side just in time to see the man he was chasing jump into a silver truck and speed off. Although he'd caught a glimpse of the man, the knit hat and neck gaiter had hidden his facial features, and simply knowing the man's approximate height and build wouldn't be enough to pick the guy out of a lineup.

Who was the man, and why had he attacked Emma? No, not Emma. Hadley. Hadley Logan. That was the name she went by now. Hopefully, Ryan hadn't scared her by calling her Emma earlier.

He picked his way back through the wooded area. Time to have a conversation with the woman he'd traveled three hundred and fifty miles to find. He'd come to tell her Troy Odom was in prison and she didn't have to hide any longer. After this, he had to wonder what she had gotten herself into in this new life of hers.

Ryan had expected this to be a happy visit. Now he wasn't so sure. Then again, maybe his timing was perfect. After all, she'd already proven her ability to disappear with a change of identity. Maybe she could do it once more. She could go back to being Emma Bryant and perhaps escape whatever danger was lurking on her doorstep in Wyoming.

Rounding the corner of the house, he stopped short. Emma sat in her vehicle with the motor running. If his truck hadn't blocked her exit, he was sure she would have been long gone. Where were the police? Had she phoned in the attack as he'd instructed?

He walked over to the driver's-side window and rapped his knuckles on the glass. Emma jumped and turned to face him, wide-eyed. Ryan motioned for her to roll down the window. She hesitated, but then lowered it an inch. He couldn't fault her for being cautious.

"I don't know if you remember me, but—"

"You have the wrong person. My name isn't Emma. I appreciate you coming to my rescue. But can you please move your vehicle so I can take my daughter somewhere safe and out of the cold?"

Daughter? He ducked and looked into the back seat. A small child was asleep in a car seat. Jessica hadn't mentioned in the letter that Emma had a daughter. The child looked to be rather young. Had Emma met someone after fleeing Troy? Was the man who'd attacked her the child's father? Maybe Ryan had stumbled into a domestic dispute.

Statistically speaking, it was possible that she'd gone from one abusive relationship to another. Her life choices weren't his business. Even so, he would not leave until the blond-haired, hazel-eyed woman with the frightened expression on her face knew Troy had finally been brought to justice and would spend the rest of his life in prison for Jessica's murder.

"You're right. It is cold out here. Get your daughter, and we'll go inside where it's warmer. I promise to protect both of you, if your husband comes back."

Shock registered on her face. "You think that was my husband? I never saw that man before in my life. And I don't know you. For all I know you're working with that guy and are just trying to trick me into trusting you."

"If that were true, why would I have told you to call nine-one-one?" He locked eyes with her, refusing to look away or blink. "You did call in the attack, didn't you?"

"Of course, I did." She swallowed. "They should be here soon. So you're free to leave."

He frowned and shrugged. "I can't go until I tell you what I came all this way to say."

"And what exactly would that be?"

"That you don't have to stay in hiding. Troy can't hurt you any longer."

She lifted a shaky hand to her throat. "Why should I believe you?"

"Because two days ago, he was sentenced to life in prison without the possibility of parole."

"Life in prison." The color drained from her face. "Who did he kill?"

Who did he kill? *Only the person who, know-*

ing she would be in danger by doing so, put her life on the line to save yours. He wanted to scream the answer, but he couldn't force the words past the lump in his throat.

Would his heart ever completely heal from the loss of the person he had thought he would spend the rest of his life loving and protecting? Probably not. At least, he could make sure she hadn't died in vain by ensuring the woman and child in front of him stayed safe.

Hadley opened her car door, lightly bumping the man's legs, and he moved to the side. "Who did Troy kill?" she asked for the second time, closing the door behind her.

"Jessica Jameson," he replied softly.

Her breath caught. Jessica had been murdered? Hadley's knees buckled, and she leaned against her car for support.

She searched his face, reading it as one would the pages of a novel, seeking to understand what was hidden beneath the surface. A subtle twitch in his jaw was the only sign he was fighting to restrain his anger. No. Not anger. Pain. A deep sadness was etched in his eyes. Sapphire-blue eyes. She'd only ever seen eyes that exact shade of blue once. In a photo of a marine wearing dress blues. The man before her was Jessica's fiancé, Ryan Vincent.

"When did…" She swallowed, but couldn't make herself say the words.

"The same night you became Hadley Logan."

A gasp escaped her.

"She told you about that?"

"Yes and no. She wrote the details in a letter to me that night. Unfortunately, the letter was never mailed. It was tucked inside a book, like she got interrupted when she was writing it and didn't want the person to see it. I didn't find it until recently."

Hadley struggled to process all of the information. Though she couldn't imagine the reason why Jessica's fiancé had tracked her down. She owed it to her friend to at least hear him out before sending him on his way. Then, once he was gone, she'd have to take her daughter and run, again. Only this time, if Troy truly was in prison, she had no clue whom she was running from. And she'd have to do a better job hiding.

"How did you find me? I didn't tell Jessica where I was going."

"Fingerprints. You were fingerprinted before being accepted into the teacher education program. And again, when you were hired for your job." He shrugged. "I have a contact in the FBI who accessed the database for me."

Okay. Good to know. She would have to reevaluate her career options and avoid any job that required fingerprints in the future.

"This is too big a conversation to have outdoors, in the cold. The police should be here soon. Let me get Sophia. We'll go inside and talk while we wait for them," she said.

As she stepped back through the front door of her home, the safety Hadley had felt the past couple of years evaporated. She took a few deep breaths and prayed her racing heartbeat wouldn't wake Sophia. Legs wobbling as she fought to tamp down the fear threatening to suffocate her, she maneuvered around the maze of books, clothes and toppled furniture, and walked down the hall. Entering Sophia's bedroom a wave of sorrow swept over her at the discovery that it had also been ransacked. She crossed over to the bed and reached with her free hand to push a pile of clothes onto the floor.

"Don't touch anything. The police will need to take pictures."

Her hand froze in midair for half a second before she continued on her mission. "I will not stand in the middle of my ravaged house and hold my sleeping daughter." The quiet life she'd fought to maintain for her daughter had been shattered, and she refused to take a back seat, following orders while her world continued to fracture. What could it matter if the T-shirts, pajamas and socks the intruder had pulled from the dresser were strewn across the bed where he'd tossed them or dumped on the floor?

She straightened and turned to find Ryan standing across the room, gaping at her. Obviously, he was a man who was used to people following his orders. Logically, she knew he was right, and she shouldn't have touched anything. However, she had vowed a long time ago that she'd always be in control of her own life. Right now it seemed the only thing she could control was giving Sophia a place to rest peacefully before her little world was turned upside down.

"Let's go talk, then you can be on your way." She lifted her head high and started for the door, her steps faltering when she spotted the broken picture frame on the dresser. Tears stung her eyes. The vandal had stolen the photo—a close-up of mother and child, laughing as they rode the carousel on the boardwalk at the beach during their summer vacation last August. Regardless of what Ryan said, Troy had to be the one behind the break-in. Who else would have wanted that picture? He must have escaped from prison.

"It's going to be okay." Ryan gently touched her shoulders and turned her toward the door. "You and your daughter are safe, and that's all that matters. Material things can be replaced."

Realistically he was right, but not all photos could be replaced. This particular snapshot had been taken by an employee at the boardwalk whose job had been to take photos for visitors to purchase as souvenirs. Even if they went back and recaptured the image, it wouldn't be the same. Sophia would be older. The sky might not be the same shade of blue and the clouds might not seem as fluffy. Unable to form coherent words, Hadley nodded and led the way down the hall and into the open living area.

"Stay here. And don't touch anything. Please." His tone softened. "I'm going to double-check the perimeter. Make sure the perp hasn't returned."

His words penetrated the haze that had descended on her brain after seeing the missing photo. "He won't come back while you're here. Troy doesn't like to have witnesses to his crimes. He's a smooth talker who comes across as an all-around good guy. He tends to reserve his dark side for the women he claims to love." Hadley hated the tremor of fear she heard in her voice. Could Ryan hear it, too?

He stepped in front of her and lifted her chin until her eyes met his. "I told you Troy is in prison. He can't hurt you."

"And why was he just sentenced, if he murdered Jessica the night I left?"

"Because he ran." Ryan shoved a hand through

his hair. "I chased him around the world. And finally caught up with him in Brazil, almost a year ago today."

A strange mixture of anger, regret and compassion bubbled up inside of her. Anger that this man had brought her past memories crashing down around her. Regret that her escape from Troy had led to Jessica's death. And compassion for everything her friend's fiancé had been through in the past six years, trying to put a killer behind bars instead of living happily ever after with the woman who had adored him. Hadley remembered the pangs of envy she'd felt whenever Jessica talked about Ryan. Their entire future had been planned out. Jessica would be an English teacher, and Ryan would leave the military and become a private security specialist.

"Did you open the security firm with Jessica's brother?"

Surprise registered on his handsome face, and he took a step backward. "Protective Instincts. Yes." He sighed. "She told you about those plans?"

"Yeah." The tears that had threatened earlier bubbled over and streamed down her face. She wiped them away with the back of her hand. "I'm so sorry helping me cost Jessica her life."

Ryan turned away from her, yanked his glasses off and pinched the bridge of his nose.

"Not your fault." His voice caught. He opened his mouth and closed it again, his jaw twitching. He visibly swallowed, looked at her and released his breath. "I'm sorry. I never meant to imply Jessica's death was your fault. There were no signs of forcible entry into her apartment that night. It's obvious she let Troy in. No one knows why she opened that door. I'm guessing she thought she could convince him to leave you alone." He shrugged. "She always acted as if she were invincible."

"Mommy. Mommy!" Sophia cried.

"I've got to check on her." Hadley hated to leave him in obvious distress, but her daughter needed her.

"Of course." He checked the time on his phone. "I'll call nine-one-one and see what's taking the officer so long, then check the perimeter. Just to be safe." He punched in the number and moved toward the kitchen island.

Sophia let out another wail, galvanizing Hadley into action. She'd taken a couple of steps down the hall when the front window shattered, a bullet hitting the picture on the wall behind where she and Ryan had been standing. It was followed quickly by a second bullet that took down a lamp, just before an engine revved and sped down the road.

Sophia screamed, and Hadley raced down the

hall, vaguely aware of Ryan moving toward the front door, gun in hand.

Dear Lord, if it's not Troy, then who is after me? And how do I escape a second time?

TWO

Ryan pushed through the front door and onto the porch in time to see a silver king cab pickup truck turn left and race down the highway. He hadn't been quick enough to get the license plate number, but it looked like the same truck the intruder had escaped in earlier. Frustrated, he let out an exasperated sigh. Hopefully, the police would get into gear and finally show up at the scene, especially since he'd been on the phone with 911 when the shots were fired. An active shooter should be more urgent than a simple breaking and entering.

He scanned the neighboring homes, looking for activity. No one was around. Did all of her neighbors work? Was there no one home who could have seen anything? He shoved the gun back into his waistband and went inside. Hadley paced in the living room, her daughter wrapped tightly in her arms. The little girl sniffled, her face buried in her mom's neck.

"Is she okay? She's not hurt, is she?"

"No. Just scared." Hadley whispered soothing words into the child's ear, bouncing as she walked, trying to get the cries to subside.

"Maybe I can help." He went over to the pair. "What did you say her name is?"

"Sophia."

The child squirmed and kicked her feet, burying her face even deeper into the hollow of her mother's neck.

"Sophia. What a pretty name." He stepped closer, and in a singsong voice, said, "Hey, hey, Sophia. Give me a smile sweet, Sophia." The sobs ceased, and giggles erupted from the tiny bundle. "Ah, there's that smile. Let me see."

A siren rent the air and the child raised her head, a look of wonder on her face. Her hazel eyes lit up, and she smiled a lopsided smile punctuated by a single dimple that looked exactly like… Troy Odom's smile. Her father.

His breath caught. Jessica hadn't mentioned in her letter that Emma was pregnant with Troy's child when they came up with the plan for her escape. But, then again, she'd been interrupted while writing the letter.

He could almost envision Troy coming to Jessica's door that night, and her hastily shoving the letter into the nearest book. In this case, a devotional book on the power of prayer. After catching Troy, Ryan had felt he was finally ready to sit down and face the emotional turmoil of sorting through the box of Jessica's belongings that her family had given him following her funeral. And he'd found the letter tucked inside the book.

Did Troy know about the girl? If he didn't, what would he do when he found out about her? Would he hurt her? No. Surely not. No matter how much the man seemed to hate women, he wouldn't resent his own daughter. Right? Besides, he was in prison. He couldn't hurt anyone, ever again. But what about Troy's family? His brother Parker, a high-powered corporate attorney, had threatened Ryan outside the courthouse on more than one occasion during the trial, and when the guilty verdict was read, he'd spewed obscenities and vowed to do whatever it took to get the judgment overturned. Now that Ryan thought about it, the build of the man he'd chased earlier was about the same as Parker's. If it was him, why had he followed Ryan across state lines? Could he have been looking to exact revenge?

Ryan had stopped by Hadley's house a couple of hours earlier. Only, she hadn't been at home, and he'd decided to take a drive and clear his mind while waiting for her to get off work. Had Parker known Ryan was visiting Emma? Or had he broken into the home simply to find out why

Ryan was there and figured it all out when he saw the picture in the bedroom? Had the picture triggered him to ransack the place? So many questions that needed answered.

The siren grew louder as a police cruiser pulled into the drive. Ryan met Hadley's eyes. "We need time to figure out if the person who did this is after Hadley or Emma. After you file the report, I'll take you and Sophia someplace safe, because I have no doubt whoever is after you will be back."

Twenty minutes later, after giving his statement, Ryan stood to the side as Hadley answered additional questions for the responding officers. One, an overweight middle-aged man who looked like his favorite stakeout spot was the local diner; the other, an overeager rookie who wanted to call in a forensic team to dust everything for prints, take cement castings of any tracks in the yard and set up a twenty-four-hour surveillance. Ryan liked the young man's spunk but didn't imagine any of his ideas would come to fruition. Eagle Creek boasted a population of less than five thousand residents. He doubted they had the equipment or man power to solve this crime or provide protection from future attacks.

He itched to jump in and tell the officers that instead of wasting their time checking for prints that would probably never materialize, they should check the whereabouts of Troy Odom's brother, but Ryan didn't have any proof Parker was behind the break-in. So instead, he gave short responses to the questions that were directed to him and counted the minutes until the officers left so he could get Hadley and her daughter somewhere safe.

The little girl sat on the floor in a corner of the living room, watching cartoons on the television and eating a snack, only occasionally casting a sneaky glance in the direction of the adults. She seemed to be taking things in stride, not overly concerned about the ransacked house or the strangers who had appeared. Hadley was signing the police report, so Ryan made his way over to the chair by the fireplace, a few feet away from the child.

Sitting down, he suddenly felt very tired. The weight of the past six years—the countless hours spent traveling the globe trying to capture Troy—along with the exhaustion of the trial, discovering Hadley's existence, tracking her down, then driving almost six hours to talk to her, followed by the events of the day all seemed to catch up with him at once. He sighed.

"You okay, mister?" a soft voice asked as he felt a tug on his shirtsleeve.

He turned his attention to the little girl with the wavy pale copper hair and hazel eyes. She was beautiful like her mother; the only obvious signs of who her father was were the dimple and lopsided smile. He'd never known those features could be so pretty, having only focused on them in recent years as traits of his enemy.

"Yes. Thank you." He didn't know how to interact with children, and it would be best for all involved if he and the child didn't bond. Maybe, if he stayed quiet, she'd go back to watching cartoons. Then he could take a few moments to acclimate to all that had happened. He looked out the front window, silently willing her to leave him alone.

Another tug on his sleeve showed the little girl had determination. Turning toward her, he bit back a grin. With a quizzical expression on her face, and one eyebrow cocked, she reminded him of his sister, Bridget. If she *was* like his sister, he wouldn't get a moment's peace until he let her have her say.

"Can I help you?" Now, why had he said that? Was that any way to talk to a child? He truly didn't know. The only young child he'd ever spent any time around was his brother Charlie's two-year-old, Jonah. But even then, there had always been another family member—grandparent, aunt or uncle—ready and willing to interact with the child.

"No, thank you." She climbed up onto the

chair and sat beside him. "You Mommy's friend? What's your name? Do you like goldfish?"

Yep, a talker. Like Bridget. Time to pick which questions to answer and which ones to dodge. There was no way he'd be able to answer the first one. He couldn't say he was friends with her mommy when he'd only met her an hour earlier, but he couldn't say he wasn't, either. The child most likely wouldn't understand the term *acquaintance*. And what was with the goldfish question? Did she have a pet? He hadn't seen a fish tank around anywhere. Maybe she'd had one but something happened to it. He didn't want to get into a discussion about where pets went when they left this earth.

He sighed, "My name is Ryan. What's your name?"

"Sophia Ann Logan." She held her hand toward him and unclenched her fingers, revealing crackers that had left orange powder all over her palm. "Do you want a Goldfish?"

Crackers. Cheese-flavored crackers shaped like fish. The little girl was offering to share her snack with him. Her sweetness touched his heart, but not enough to encourage him to eat the offered snack.

"No, thank you. I don't like them."

The little girl's eyes welled with tears, and her lower lip quivered.

Way to go, making a child cry. This was why he tended to avoid children. Not that he didn't like them, but he didn't know how to communicate with them. To be honest, he didn't know how to communicate with most people. Other than his family and his business partner, Lincoln Jameson. They accepted him the way he was. A loner who preferred the company of his tech gadgets and computers over most people he'd ever met.

"What don't you like?"

Uh-oh, moms tended to take offense to anyone who made their children cry. And moms who have had their home broken into and been shot at were probably even more sensitive to anyone upsetting their little one.

"Goldfish." He and the child said in unison.

Ryan stood—instinctively picking the child up as he did so—and faced Hadley. "Look, can we save this discussion for later? It's a misunderstanding. Right now, we have more pressing issues to concern ourselves with." He was acutely aware of the child looking back and forth between them. Thrusting Sophia into her mom's arms, he continued, "Get her settled. Then go pack, quickly, so we can get out of here."

Getting them to safety immediately was as much for Ryan's sake as it was for theirs. He needed to be in a place where he could take a few minutes to think and process the events of the day, and figure out if he had inadvertently led danger to Hadley's doorstep.

Hadley tamped down her annoyance that Ryan had upset Sophia. She would not let her child see her arguing with a stranger.

"Sophia, Mommy needs to talk to this man—"

"Ryan," Sophia supplied.

Hadley glared at him. He'd been busy. She didn't want him disrupting her daughter's world any more than necessary.

She kissed Sophia on the nose. "Yes, *Mr.* Ryan." It was important for her daughter to learn to address adults with appropriate titles and show respect. "Now, I need you to sit right here on the couch and finish watching your cartoon. Mommy and *Mr.* Ryan will be right over there at the kitchen island, talking. Okay?"

"Okay, Mommy." Sophia reached for her favorite stuffed animal—a panda bear named Mr. Bamboo—so Hadley scooped it off the coffee table and handed it to her before walking across the room.

Please, Lord, help me keep Sophia safe.

The first six months of her life as Hadley Logan had been spent as an unwed mother-to-be. Alone and scared, she had barely slept, and anytime she went outside the tiny apartment she had rented in Casper, she looked over her shoulder every five seconds, convinced Troy had found her.

Once Sophia was born, she'd been so busy taking care of an infant that she'd slowly stopped looking for danger lurking in the shadows. Then she'd gotten the teaching job here in Eagle Creek and moved her little family seventy-five miles north.

Going from Denver with a population of nearly three million to Casper with a population of 60,000 to Eagle Creek with a population of 4,709 had required stepping outside her comfort zone. In the larger city, she'd been able to hide in the crowd, but in Eagle Creek, everyone quickly learned her name. And where she lived. Making it easy for anyone to find her. Why had she let her guard down?

"You need to pack a suitcase for you and the child. I'll take you somewhere safe while we figure out who's behind the break-in and shooting," Ryan said, interrupting her thoughts.

"We both know who's behind it." She busied herself fixing Sophia a cup of juice. "I've been meaning to have one of those video doorbells installed but never got around to it. If I had, we'd have pictures to prove who it was." She took the drink and sat it on the table beside Sophia, caressed her hair and returned to the kitchen area.

Hadley had to figure out how to get rid of Ryan. She didn't want to go into hiding with a man she had just met today. Besides, if Jessica had been killed for helping her escape, anyone else who helped her would also be in danger. There was no way she was going to let another person put himself in harm's way. Not even a former military guy.

"Look, my daughter and I aren't going anywhere with you. You're a stranger to us."

"That's not exactly true, is it? Though we never met face-to-face before today, Jessica told you all about me. You already admitted as much earlier when you asked about Protective Instincts." He raised an eyebrow as if to dare her to try and convince him she didn't know exactly who he was, his background and why he might well be the only one who could keep her and Sophia safe.

"Has anyone ever told you that you have a very expressive face?" he continued. "I could tell the exact moment you recognized me. I'm guessing you saw the photo collage that filled the wall behind Jessica's sofa." A smile lifted the corner of his mouth. "It took me hours to get every frame hung to her satisfaction. I remember halfway through the project I tried to convince her there were too many pictures, but she said every photo was a memory frozen in time and she couldn't leave any out.

"I imagine the photo that's missing from the frame in Sophia's room was a memory, too." He sobered and leaned in close. "The only way to ensure whoever did this doesn't hurt your daughter is for you to trust me."

Her chest tightened and she inhaled sharply. From the day she became Hadley, she'd known she had a greater chance of being struck by lightning, twice, than she did of keeping her past from catching up to her.

"Until today, no one knew Troy had a daughter." A tear slipped down her cheek. She hated herself for the show of weakness, but she also knew herself well enough to know it would be the last tear she shed over the loss of her peaceful life in Eagle Creek.

Swiping the tear away with the back of her hand, she straightened. The French doors leading to the patio provided a clear view of the officers snapping pictures of shoe prints with their cell phones. She hoped they were able to get clear photos, because what little evidence had been left behind would soon disappear. Snow was in the air. The projected blizzard would dump close to a foot of the wet stuff on the area overnight, permanently erasing the prints. "Should I check with the officers before I start packing?"

"Let me." He strode to the patio with a casual confidence and then leaned halfway out the door. Muffled conversation followed. He nodded, closed the door and snapped the lock into place before rejoining her. "Officer Michaels said they're finished inside. He also said he thinks it's *wise* for you and the child to stay with a friend tonight and to pack whatever you need."

She nodded, resigned to do as he wished…at least for the time being.

Ten minutes later, she'd packed a small rolling suitcase and backpack with several changes of clothes and a few books and toys to keep Sophia entertained. One last thing to pack, and she would be ready to go.

Hadley knelt on the floor and pulled the black fireproof lockbox out from under her bed. Her fingers flew over the keypad. When she heard the soft click, she tugged open the lid, thankful she'd been diligent about hoarding away a hundred dollars a month, even in the leanest months. That, along with her last two tax refunds, had left her a nice amount of cash for an occasion such as this one.

Her hand on the lid, she only hesitated half a second before retrieving her and Sophia's passports and birth certificates and slipping them into the front pocket of the backpack. Just in case they needed to flee farther this time.

THREE

"You're sure Troy hasn't escaped and his brother hasn't left the state today?" Ryan had a hard time believing Troy wasn't the one behind the break-in and shooting, even from behind bars. The odds someone else had it in for Hadley and had chosen to attack the same day he appeared seemed very low to him.

"Troy was transferred to the state penitentiary yesterday, without incident. After his arrival he was placed in solitary confinement on suicide watch. As for Parker Odom, according to his secretary he was in court all day. I can't verify if she's telling the truth until morning, when the clerk's office reopens." Lincoln sighed. "In the meantime, we'll stake out Parker's residence. Now get your friend and her child to the safe house. And stay put until we figure out who's after her."

Though he didn't like the idea of hiding out and waiting for others to catch the shooter, Ryan didn't take offence at his friend's command. At

Protective Instincts, Lincoln's role was to protect. He was in charge of the bodyguards and all communication with their clients. Ryan's role was to oversee the installation of security systems and behind-the-scenes issues that included using his computer skills to find things people would like to leave hidden. Since he never traveled without a laptop, he'd still be able to do his part to help track down the suspect.

"Ryan?" Lincoln pulled him from his thoughts.

"Yeah?"

"I know you want to be the one chasing after the bad guys, but you have the most important job of all. If Jessica was willing to sacrifice her life to save Hadley and her child..." Linc's voice faltered.

"We owe it to her memory to see that she didn't die in vain," Ryan said, filling in the blank. A lump formed in his throat, and he forcefully swallowed. Ryan felt like a heel. Jessica was Linc's younger sister. Linc grieved her loss, and anything that would be a reminder of the nature of her death would be hard on him, too. "Got it. I'll take care of things on this end. In the meantime, you get eyes on Parker. And whatever you do, don't let him out of your sight."

Hadley came out of her bedroom, wearing a backpack and pulling a small rolling suitcase while carrying a rolled-up blanket under her arm.

Time to hit the road. "Linc, I've gotta go. I'll check in once we get to our destination." He disconnected the call and slipped the phone into his back pocket, then headed down the hall to help Hadley with her luggage.

"Sophia fell asleep on the couch about two seconds after you left the room."

"I'm not surprised. Her nap was interrupted. Remember? Let me grab a few snacks out of the cabinet, and we can go. We don't want a hungry child on our hands." She turned toward the kitchen. "If you want, you can move the car seat from my vehicle to yours while I finish up here."

"Deputy Newton already took care of that." He reached for the cloth sack she had filled with juice boxes and an assortment of granola bars and fruit snacks. "You carry the munchkin. I'll get the bags. The officers are waiting outside. They're going to follow us to the county line to ensure we don't run into trouble."

Her face solemn, she nodded and scooped Sophia up into her arms. In a matter of minutes, the luggage had been loaded and the child was strapped snuggly into her car seat, her stuffed animal in her arms and the blanket tucked around her.

The SUV was engulfed in silence as Ryan focused on making his way down the curvy mountain road. Twenty minutes later, he lifted a hand to bid the officers farewell and turned south onto I-25.

"We should be able to get a couple of hotel rooms in Casper," Hadley said, her first words since they began their journey.

"Change of plans." He glanced in the rear-view mirror. At the moment, traffic was light and none of the vehicles jumped out at him as being suspicious. "Linc thought it would be better if we headed to Colorado."

Hadley shifted in her seat and turned to face him. "Why?"

Her tone was resigned, not angry. He was impressed with her ability to go with the flow and not become hysterical or demanding.

"Linc's grandfather left him a house in northern Colorado. It's situated where you can see for miles in every direction, making it very hard for someone to sneak up on us. Plus, last summer, Linc and I installed the best security system on the market with the intentions of using the place as a safe house if the need ever arose."

"While I appreciate the thought you've put into our safety, we can't go to Colorado."

"I told you, Troy is—"

"It's not about Troy. My mom is here. In an assisted living facility in Foster Falls, a small town outside of Casper. I can't leave her."

The surprises just kept coming. He had discovered an obituary for Emma's father but hadn't been able to locate her mother. Now he knew why. She had gone into hiding with her daughter and granddaughter. "That's no problem. I'll call Linc and have him send a bodyguard to relocate your mom somewhere safe."

"No. You don't understand. My mom has Alzheimer's. I can't have her routine upset. I visit her twice a week and read to her. Most of the time, she doesn't know who I am, but the nurses say that she looks for me on those days. Once, when Sophia was sick, I missed a visit and my mom mentally shut down for days, refusing to eat or get out of bed. Besides, with Troy locked up, there's no one else who would want to hurt me. Which means we're probably overreacting. It was just a random burglary that I interrupted."

Linc knew she was grasping at straws and doubted she even believed what she was saying. He'd seen the look on her face when she saw the missing photo, and while he hated to point out the obvious flaw in her theory, he needed her to take the situation more seriously. "Okay, then, what about the drive-by shooting?"

"I don't know. Maybe he thought I could identify him, and it was a warning to keep my mouth shut…" Her voice faded as she turned and looked out the back window.

Ryan kept his gaze focused on the road ahead.

He didn't need to see her face to know she didn't believe her own words and was searching for shadows of her past, wondering if she could outrun them again. How was she going to feel when he told her he suspected Troy's brother Parker was behind the attack?

He hated himself for leading danger to her. As much as he didn't like facing that fact, he knew he was responsible for the events of the day. If he'd simply stayed parked in front of her house and waited for her to arrive home, he might have been able to stop the break-in. Yep. No coincidences today. He, Ryan Vincent, had led Troy's hitman or his brother to Hadley's home. Now he had to do the one thing he hadn't been able to do for Jessica. He had to keep Hadley and Sophia alive.

Another look in the rearview mirror showed the child was still sleeping. Good. Maybe he could get answers to some of his questions.

Might as well start with the one that had played on repeat in his brain for the last four months while he was on his quest to find what happened to Emma Bryant, never dreaming his search would lead him to Hadley and her daughter, Sophia.

"Either way, if we go to Colorado or stop somewhere in Wyoming for the night, we have a bit of a drive ahead of us. Why don't you use this time to tell me about the events that led up to you and Jessica hatching the plan to fake your death and how you executed it? Also, did Troy know you were pregnant when you ran?"

Wanting to delay her answer, Hadley twisted in her seat to look at her daughter. Sophia was sleeping peacefully. Her stuffed panda bear, Mr. Bamboo, had fallen from her grasp and lay on the floor of the vehicle. Stretching, Hadley got two fingers on the panda and, with one quick tug on his fur, plopped him back onto the seat where he'd be within Sophia's grasp when she awoke.

"Ow." She rubbed her side and tried to relieve a muscle spasm as she eased back into her seat.

"Are you okay? Do I need to find a place to pull over so you can stretch?" Concern punctuated Ryan's words.

"No… I'm fine…just a catch in my side." She looked out the window, trying to get her bearings. "How long will it take to reach the safe house?"

"Um… I'd say about six hours, if we were going there. But I've decided you're right. We can find a hotel for the night and develop a plan on how to proceed. After all, the main goal is to make sure everyone stays safe, your mom included."

Relief washed over her. "Thank you."

He offered a half smile. "It's the right thing to do. But we're not staying in Casper. We'll try to find a hotel about thirty minutes from there. Some place no one would think to look for you. And I won't take you to see your mom unless I feel like it's safe."

Hadley leaned back and suppressed a sigh. She had always known the peace she'd felt the last couple of years couldn't last.

"Are you going to continue to ignore my earlier question? I think I deserve answers, don't you? A chance to understand the thought process for your charade as Hadley." His tone was matter-of-fact, not accusatory.

The suppressed sigh escaped. No point putting off the inevitable.

"Troy knew I was pregnant but thought I'd gotten the abortion he'd demanded. He doesn't know about Sophia. Or he didn't..." Why had the intruder taken the photo of her and Sophia? Would she be able to keep her daughter safe?

"Jessica and I met the last semester of college. We were doing our teaching internship in the same high school. She saw Troy pick me up a few times. Then one day, she noticed some bruising on my upper arm. Troy and I had had a disagreement, and when I tried to walk away, he grabbed me." A phantom pain gripped her biceps, a memory from the first time the man she thought loved her had threatened her life.

"Upper arm where the bruises could be covered by clothing," Ryan whispered, and she wondered if he was remembering a time Jessica had similar wounds, inflicted by Troy.

"Jessica cornered me in the teacher's lounge," Hadley continued, choosing not to acknowledge his words. Shame washed over her as she mentally counted the number of times she had worn long-sleeve shirts to hide marks, although at the time, she hadn't thought of it as abuse. Troy hadn't hit her. He'd just hold her in place, his grip biting into her flesh, as he proceeded to tell her all the things she'd done wrong that day. Soft-spoken, menacing words. No yelling.

To an outsider looking in, she was sure it looked intimate, a couple in love having a whispered, private conversation. He was always apologetic about the bruises. Sorry he'd held her so tightly. It wasn't his fault she bruised so easily, or so he'd said. Every single time.

She swallowed, forcing herself to think without feeling. "Jessica told me she and Troy dated for six months freshman year of college and how controlling he had been during their relationship. That his temper had become increasingly worse over time and he'd become physically abusive. Which led to you and Lincoln stepping in and encouraging her to obtain the restraining order against him."

"Actually, we did a bit more than that."

"What do you mean?"

Ryan shrugged. "When we saw the bruises, we paid Troy a visit at the frat house. To let him know that we'd be around to keep an eye on him and make sure Jessica was safe from harm."

"She never told me about that."

"Because she never knew." He spared her a quick glance. "Please, continue. What were your thoughts when Jessica shared her story of dating Troy?"

"Although I recognized a lot of the behaviors she described, I didn't want to believe her. It had been three years since they'd dated. I convinced myself Troy had matured since then and wasn't the same person… Then he was late picking me up one afternoon. Jessica decided to sit with me while I waited. He saw us talking, and when I got into the car, he became irrational. We argued the entire ride home." Mortification enveloped her, and she felt a flush sweep up her neck and cheeks. Even though she knew God had forgiven her sins when she became a Christian, her past still brought shame.

"You don't have to tell me everything. Just the things you think are relevant." Ryan's words pulled her back to the present.

"It's okay. You might as well know." She rubbed her arms, chilled in spite of the warmth flowing from the heat vents. "We lived in a two-story condo. All evening, Troy kept hounding me to tell him what 'lies' Jessica had been filling my head with. He kept screaming and belittling me. I packed an overnight bag so I could go to a hotel. To think. And to give Troy time to cool down.

"He confronted me on the second-floor landing. Said I wasn't leaving. I was his property."

"Why, that no good—" Ryan gave her an apologetic half smile. "Sorry. Continue."

"When I tried to go around him, he grabbed me. And I fell down the stairs. I can't say if he pushed me or if it was an accident—"

"That was no accident!"

Sophia moaned in the back seat, and Hadley turned to soothe her. "Shhh… It's okay." She rubbed her daughter's leg and tucked her fuzzy blankie closer.

Once Sophia was settled, Hadley sank back into her seat. Closing her eyes, she exhaled softly. Couldn't the man control his emotions and let her finish telling him what happened?

"I'm sorry. Didn't mean to disturb the kid." He glanced at her, his face shrouded in shadows as darkness began to settle around them, the sun sinking lower behind the mountains. "Please, continue. I promise to keep my opinions to myself."

While he didn't say it, she could almost hear the words *for now* tacked on to the end of his sentence.

She shook her head and sighed, all the energy leaving her body. Long-suppressed memories clawed to the surface. "In a nutshell… My name was changed when I was three years old. I never shared the information with anyone. When I decided to disappear, Jessica thought it would be simplest if I used my birth name. Since Troy didn't know about my name change, he wouldn't know to search for me as Hadley Logan." She sighed. He was sure to want more details but there was no way she could continue. Not just yet.

"I don't want to frighten you," Ryan said in a terrifyingly calm voice, his gaze focused on something in the rearview mirror. "But it looks like your intruder found us."

"What? No." She twisted in her seat to look over her shoulder. A speeding silver truck, still a good distance behind them, passed the vehicles trailing them one by one, zeroing in on Ryan's vehicle like a guided missile. "What are we going to do? There's nowhere to hide."

Fear gripped her, and her body trembled. What she'd gone through six years ago had seemed like the worst thing she could ever experience, but the unknown of what she was running from now could in fact be much worse.

FOUR

"The goal is to stay ahead of him and not let him catch us," Ryan said calmly, as he mentally ran through their options. According to the last sign he'd seen, the next exit should be coming up soon. All he had to do was keep as many vehicles as he could between his SUV and the truck, and then exit without giving the guy a chance to follow them. Easy-peasy. Or so he hoped.

He pressed down on the accelerator and passed the minivan they'd been behind for the last fifteen minutes. Mimicking his move, the guy in the silver truck sped past another vehicle, working his way closer to them.

"He's weaving in and out of traffic, going dangerously fast on roads with snow and ice… He's getting closer. Only one vehicle between us," Hadley said, giving a play-by-play.

Ryan knew she was trying to be helpful but her imitation of a sportscaster grated on his nerves like fingernails on a chalkboard. Up ahead, a fast-food sign declared the next exit was in three miles. The vehicles behind him were at least half a mile back. If he didn't want the driver of the silver truck to follow him at the exit, he'd have to trick him into thinking he wasn't exiting.

Ryan tightened his grip on the steering wheel. "Okay, this is it. Turn around and sit."

"But—"

"Do it. Now!" He barked a little more harshly than intended. As a former officer in the Marine Corps, he was used to giving orders in short directives to military personnel who understood the urgency of the situation. But that was no excuse to yell. "Sorry."

"It's okay. I understand." She did as he instructed and then grasped the grab bar located above the passenger door, as if bracing for a crash. "Just don't take any unnecessary measures to evade the guy. Remember my child is in this vehicle."

Did she think he was a rookie? He would never do anything to purposefully put her child in danger. But if he didn't do something fast, they would all be in danger. Ryan clenched his jaws and reminded himself she was scared and needed some sense of control.

There was an eighteen-wheeler ahead of him. If he could pass it and take the exit at the last second, maybe the guy in the silver truck would shoot on past and not be able to follow them. Increasing his speed, he narrowed the distance between him and the eighteen-wheeler. A sign indicating the next exit was in one mile flashed by. He only had one mile to make his move. Switching lanes, he pressed harder on the accelerator.

"What are you doing? Aren't we taking that exit?"

"Trust me," he said, glancing in the rearview mirror.

"Come on. Nothing's stopping you. Follow me," Ryan urged the driver of the silver truck. As if on cue, the guy roared up behind him, inches between their bumpers.

Ryan surged a few feet ahead of the semi, blocking the silver truck behind him. They were nearing the exit. This was it. One. Two. Three. He pressed down on the gas and darted toward the exit, cutting across in front of the eighteen-wheeler.

Hadley's scream mingled with the semi's horn.

Jolted awake from the commotion, Sophia burst into tears. "Mommy!"

Tuning out the background noise, Ryan watched as the silver truck sped on by, blocked from following them by the eighteen-wheeler. He released a sigh and lifted his foot off the gas pedal, allowing his vehicle to decelerate. Thankfully, the exit was flat and straight.

"It's okay. We're okay," he repeated over and over soothingly, until Hadley's screams quieted and Sophia's wails turned to sniffles. "I'm sorry I scared you both."

"Did…did you lose him?" Hadley said, her voice quivering.

"For now. But I'm sure he'll take the next exit and circle back as quickly as possible, so we need to figure out a plan fast." He pulled to a stop at the end of the exit. "I have no clue where we are."

"This is the exit for Foster Falls. Where my mom lives in the nursing home."

Of all places for him to exit. He hoped the guy after them wasn't aware of Hadley's connection to this area. Ryan needed to find a place to pull over and call Lincoln and have him locate a room for them at a hotel some distance from Foster Falls. Hopefully, if the guy chasing them couldn't find them when he circled back, he'd return to Eagle Creek or wherever he came from, allowing them a chance to hole up some place and figure out who the guy was and why he was after Hadley.

"Which way are we going?" Hadley asked.

"Good question. The guy in the truck will probably expect us to continue south, so that's out. Turning around and heading north would also be risky because the guy—if he's from

Eagle Creek—may decide to call it a day and go home. The way he drives, we'd run the risk of him catching us, especially if traffic slows due to the increased snowfall." He sighed. "So, looks like we go east or west…"

"Are you always so analytical?"

What a strange question. Wasn't it good to analyze situations like this? He turned to her, taking in her raised eyebrow and thoughtful expression. "Yes. And it's served me well through the years."

A car horn sounded behind them, and he startled. The minivan he'd passed earlier sat behind him, the right blinker flashing. The driver tooted the horn again, urging him to move.

Ryan activated his blinker and turned left. "West it is."

Fifteen minutes later, he sat in his vehicle outside a gas station in the middle of nowhere, waiting for Hadley and Sophia to return from the restroom. He had filled his gas tank and then pulled his SUV into a parking space in front of the store, his eyes glued to the door. Pulling up Lincoln's number on the touchscreen on the dashboard, he pressed the call button.

Lincoln answered on the second ring. "Ryan, where are you?"

"Hello to you, too, buddy." Ryan laughed. Lincoln had always been one to get straight to the point even when answering a phone call.

"Sorry. Hello. Is everything okay?"

"For the moment, but our shooter found us. We had to take an unexpected exit and now we're somewhere on Highway 26."

"I'm pulling you up on the tracking app now..." Linc fell silent and Ryan waited, not wanting to disrupt his concentration. "Okay, found you. What's the plan? Are you going to loop around and work your way back to the interstate or stick to back roads? There's a junction about five miles east with a highway that runs south."

"We've decided to stay in Wyoming for the night. Hadley's mom is in a nursing home nearby and Hadley wants to visit her tomorrow."

"Do you think that's a good idea?"

"Not really. Which is why I'm still weighing the options." Hadley and Sophia exited the store and headed his way. "Look, I've gotta go. Let me know if you find us a couple of rooms for the night."

He disconnected the call and looked at the sky. The weather worried him, and he wasn't sure what he'd do if they couldn't find rooms for the night. He had an emergency solar blanket and a sleeping bag he kept in his vehicle during the winter months in case he ever got stranded, but he prayed they didn't have to use them.

Snowflakes pelted the windshield. Ryan increased the speed of the wipers, and the hypnotic swishing sound was magnified by the silence that had gripped the vehicle.

The snowfall had steadily increased in volume, and mounds of snow and slush had begun to cover the highway, slowing traffic almost to a standstill. They needed to find a motel, soon.

He was glad he'd called Lincoln earlier and asked him to locate them a safe place to stay for the night.

A quick glance in the rearview mirror verified Sophia had fallen asleep watching a cartoon on her tablet. Ryan didn't know much about children, but he suspected when they got settled at a hotel, the little girl would be ready to run wide-open.

"The man who raised me, who I believed was my father, wasn't," Hadley said quietly, startling him with her sudden admission. "My mom never told me about my biological father, and I never told her or my dad I knew their secret. Actually, Jessica's the only person I ever told, until now."

"Then how do you know—"

"When I was fifteen, I was snooping in my parents' room looking for my Christmas presents—I really wanted a cell phone that year. Instead of a phone, I found a metal box with old papers in it, including two birth certificates. One of them I'd used to obtain my learner's permit. It listed my name, Emma Ann Bryant, and the names of both my parents, Donna May Logan and Henry Wilson Bryant. The other birth certificate listed my name as Emma Hadley Logan, mother… Donna May Logan and father…unknown."

Ryan resisted the urge to hurl questions at her. If she felt like she was being interrogated, she'd clam up. Best to let her tell the story in her own way, in her own time. Focusing on the road, he waited.

"In a way, the secret was a blessing. As much as I loved Henry Bryant—and I will forever be grateful he was my dad—having a second birth certificate enabled me to leave my life as Emma Bryant and start over as Hadley Logan."

"I'm confused why you decided to jump straight to disappearing. Did you go to the police? File a restraining order?"

Hadley scoffed. "Jessica had a restraining order, and it didn't protect her, did it?"

Ryan flinched as if she'd slapped him. Restraining orders weren't perfect by any means. He knew that all too well.

"I'm sorry. I didn't mean that the way it sounded."

"It's okay. You only spoke the truth. May I ask why you felt your only option was to disappear? Was it because of Sophia?"

"The night Troy pushed me down the stairs, the ER doctor told me I was pregnant. Troy's response was, *We'll have to take care of that problem immediately.*"

"Wait a minute." Ryan took a deep breath and lowered his voice, "Troy was in the hospital room with you? Why hadn't he been arrested?"

"I was unconscious when the ambulance arrived, but apparently, Troy had staged the scene to look like I had fallen down the stairs while carrying a laundry basket full of clothes." She sighed. "When I came to, he was sitting beside my bed acting like a loving, concerned boyfriend, mainly for the benefit of the hospital staff. The doctor came in and asked if I wanted Troy to leave before he discussed my condition. Troy squeezed my hand and gave me a look that made it clear it would be a mistake to say or do anything that made him look bad, so I just shook my head."

"His demand that you terminate the pregnancy was the reason you thought the only option was to run?"

Hadley nodded, "I was afraid he'd hurt me if

he knew I'd defied him. And I couldn't put my baby's life in jeopardy."

Instinctively, he reached over and squeezed her hand. "It's okay. Sophia is safe, and we're going to make sure she stays safe."

"Thank you." Hadley pulled her hand free. "The way Jessica talked about you I know you'd never do anything to put us in danger."

His chest tightened, and he caught his breath. How would she take the news if it turned out he had led Parker to her? "Did you ever meet Troy's broth—"

His phone rang and Linc's name flashed on the screen. Hitting the answer button, Ryan said, "Hi, Linc. Please, tell me you found us a place for the night. This storm seems to be gearing up to be a doozy."

"I did. It's a small motel about five miles off the highway. I'm texting you the address now." A ding sounded to indicate the message had come through. "The snowstorm is forcing a lot of people to stop for the night. I was able to get the last two rooms. They aren't adjoining, but the desk clerk assured me they were relatively close to one another."

Ryan met Hadley's gaze. "It's okay. At least we'll be someplace warm. Thanks, buddy." He disconnected the call. "I'm sorry he couldn't get adjoining rooms. I wanted to be close so you'd feel safe and hopefully get a restful night's sleep."

"It's okay. Like you said, at least we'll be warm."

Hadley fell silent again. Ryan felt like a heel putting her through the turmoil of reliving the events leading up to her disappearance.

Lord, I pray the break-in today wasn't because of me. I don't think I could bear being responsible for adding to this woman's pain.

"Please, continue. I need to understand how you were able to just completely disappear."

"It was easier than I imagined it would be. First, I picked up my mom from the nursing home, after telling them I could no longer afford their services and would be taking care of her myself. Next, I drove to a remote area by a river where Jessica met us. Put my car in neutral and pushed it down the side of the embankment. Then, Jessica drove my mother and me to the train station, and we boarded a train to Salt Lake City. After a week there, we rented a car and drove to Cheyenne." She smiled. "Even being on the run, that was the best trip I've taken with my mom in a long time. I don't know why, if it was the excitement of the adventure or what, but she was more lucid during those two weeks than I'd seen her in the three years prior. Or the six years since. I almost convinced myself that she didn't need to be in a nursing home any longer and that I could keep her with me." She paused and he heard her take a deep breath. "I was wrong."

Ryan made a mental note to check out the security of the nursing home tomorrow. If he took Hadley and Sophia to visit. *If? You know you will. If Jessica's death and nearly losing Bridget to a serial killer last year have taught you anything, it is the importance of family. You can't expect Hadley to go into hiding without giving her a chance to see her mom. And say goodbye.*

He prayed taking her to say goodbye to her mom wouldn't be a mistake that cost all of them their lives.

FIVE

The quiet of the morning engulfed Hadley as she watched the people outside loading their vehicles and preparing to continue their journey. Ryan had sent her a text twenty minutes earlier to see if she was awake. Then he'd told her he was going in search of food and would bring breakfast to her room, which Hadley had been thankful for because it allowed her the quiet time that she was accustomed to each morning. She had made a strong cup of coffee with the in-room coffee maker, then she'd opened the blinds and pulled the only chair in the room over to the window so she could watch the sunrise and have her alone time with God.

After being awake until midnight, Sophia was still sleeping soundly, tangled in the covers in the center of the bed they had shared, blissfully unaware her mother had only gotten a few hours' rest.

Hadley sighed. *Oh, to be a child again and not have the weight of the world on your shoulders. Sleep as long as you can, little one, as I can't guarantee how peaceful, or safe, you'll feel over the next few days. Though I promise to do everything in my power to keep you out of danger.*

Hadley inhaled the scent of the coffee and took a sip as she watched her daughter's chest rise and fall. *Dear Lord, please help me keep Sophia safe.*

There was a knock at the door. She froze and listened. Ryan had a key. He'd requested two copies of keys for both rooms so they would each have the other's room key in case of emergency. Why would he knock? Had the man in the truck found them? She searched frantically for something to use as a weapon. Sophia's stuffed panda lay on the floor at her feet. She kicked it aside and made her way to the closet. The coat hangers were attached to the rod. That wouldn't work.

Muffled words and scraping sounds came from the other side of the door. An intruder wouldn't make that much noise, would they?

She tiptoed to the door. Pressing her hand against the wood, she peeked through the peephole, and smiled. Ryan, a brown paper bag tucked under his neck and held in place by his chin, balanced three carryout meal containers in one hand, which also had a drink carrier dangling from its fingers, while trying to extract his keycard from his wallet with the other hand.

Unlocking the dead bolt and swinging the door wide, she laughed. "Why didn't you say anything?"

He grasped the paper bag with the hand that held his wallet, raised his head and offered her a half smile with a shrug. "I was trying not to wake the kid."

"Well, you almost gave me a heart attack." She took the drink carrier and two of the carry-out containers and crossed to the small desk. "I thought you were the guy in the truck."

"I don't think he'd knock, do you?"

"Honestly, I don't know. He might knock and hope I'd think it was housekeeping or something. I don't have much—" She swallowed the rest of the sentence and took a few steadying breaths.

Ryan put the items he carried onto the desk and placed his hand on her shoulder. "Hey, are you okay? I'm really sorry I frightened you."

Hadley shook her head. "I was about to say, I didn't have much experience thinking like an evil person, but that isn't true, is it? I had to think like Troy to escape him, didn't I?" She took a step back and looked him in the eyes. "Looks like I let my guard down too soon. I better start thinking like the person after me, or I'll never be able to stay a step ahead of them."

Ryan's blue eyes deepened to a dark sapphire. "True. But you're not alone this time."

He pulled the chair back to its rightful place at the desk and motioned for her to sit. "Now eat, before everything gets cold."

Picking up one of the carryout containers, he took off its lid and then put it to the side before opening the next one, which he placed in front of her. Mounds of eggs, sausage, hash browns and biscuits and gravy greeted her. The smells wafted upward, tickling her nose, and her stomach growled. Ryan laughed and dumped the contents of the brown paper bag onto the desk. Utensils encased in plastic, napkins, French vanilla creamer, butter, and packets of jam and syrup scattered out before her.

Laughing, she picked up one of the utensils sets and tore into it, freeing the fork and tiny packets of salt and pepper. Soon, she had a forkful of eggs in her mouth. "Mmm." She swallowed and eyed the bodyguard standing over her. "This is good. Aren't you going to eat?"

"Yep." He snagged the other container and sat on the corner of the bed, balancing it on his knee.

They ate in silence, and she tried to concentrate on the food and ignore the awkward feeling of eating with a virtual stranger in a hotel room.

She'd just finished her coffee when Sophia sat up and smiled.

"Good morning, Mommy," Sophia said, pushing her tangled hair out of her face.

"Good morning, Sunshine." Hadley crossed over to the bed and held out her arms.

"Does she always wake up this happy?" Ryan asked in awe.

Sophia's eyes widened and her lips formed an O. She'd obviously not expected to find Ryan in their room. "Good morning, mister." Turning back to Hadley, Sophia dove off the bed and into her arms, burying her face in Hadley's shoulder.

She kissed her daughter's head and smiled at Ryan, who stood staring. "Yes, every single morning. She is a ray of sunshine. It can be annoying when I've had a really bad night and not slept well, but it's also a blessing because she motivates me to be a better person."

"I'm hungry," Sophia whispered into Hadley's neck.

"Did you get pancakes?" she asked Ryan as she shifted Sophia out of her arms and onto the chair and pulled the unopened Styrofoam container toward her.

"Yes, ma'am, as requested. I also picked up syrup and an assortment of jellies."

Hadley tore the pancakes into strips and opened one of the small tubs of syrup so Sophia could dip the pancake. "Eat up, sweetie. After you finish, we'll wash up and go visit Nonna."

Sophia nodded, her mouth full and her cheeks puffed out like a chipmunk storing up for winter.

"We've really got to talk this through," Ryan insisted.

"I know you only want to keep us safe, but we've not seen the guy since you pulled that race car driver maneuver last night and lost him. Besides, he isn't likely to know about my mom anyway. Only the people who have interacted with her at the nursing home know of her existence. Troy thinks she's dead, and I've never mentioned her to any of my colleagues or acquaintances in Wyoming. What would have been the point? It's not like they could meet her anyway."

"You make valid points, but without knowing who is after you, we can't rule out anything."

"Even so, I think we'll be safe at a nursing home." Hadley gave him her don't-argue-with-me teacher face and started to gather their belongings, preparing to leave the safety of the motel, conscious of the bodyguard's watchful eyes following her every move.

He might not like her insisting on seeing her mother, but he'd have to get over it. She'd fought too hard to get to a place where she could raise her child and provide the needed assistance to her mother. After leaving her previous life behind and having to start over with no friends, no help and no stability, she wouldn't walk away from this life as easily. No, she wouldn't give up what she had built without a fight.

Ryan could feel his frustration bubbling over. Why did Hadley have to be so difficult? Keeping her and Sophia safe was his biggest priority. Nothing else. He understood her need to have some sense of control in situations like this, but insisting on seeing a parent who might not even know they were there when someone was chasing her and her daughter seemed like a risk that shouldn't be taken.

The sound of water running, mixed with Sophia's giggles, drifted through the bathroom door, and he sighed. *Tackle one thing at a time, Vincent.*

He would wait until they were in the vehicle and the child was occupied with a video on her tablet or something before having a discussion with Hadley about the need for extra caution and weighing the pros and cons of every decision. In the meantime, he could check in with Lincoln and get the latest update on Parker's whereabouts.

Taking a few slow, steady breaths, he picked up his phone off the nightstand and punched in his partner's number.

"I was just about to call you," Linc said in typical style without even a hello. "Adeline took the first shift watching Parker's house last night. He didn't show up until midnight. It would have been tight, but it's possible he could have broken into Emma's home and—"

"Hadley."

"What?" Ryan turned to look at the woman behind him with the stern look on her face.

"My. Name. Is. Hadley. Hadley Logan," she enunciated each word.

"My name is Sophia Ann Logan." Sophia peeked at him from behind her mother's legs. Her wet hair hung in ringlets and dripped onto the floor.

He mentally kicked himself for not being more cautious. Even though Ryan had purposefully not put the phone on speaker, he should have known Hadley would be able to hear Linc since he had a commanding voice that carried, no matter how softly he tried to speak. Without taking his eyes off the mother-daughter duo, Ryan said into the phone, "Linc, I'll have to call you back."

"Okay."

"No," Hadley said.

"What's going on there?" Linc asked.

"Hadley—by the way, that's her preferred name—and her daughter walked into the room."

"Oh…"

"Look, there's no need for you to stop your conversation. This is about me—us—after all. I should be allowed to be part of the discussion. Shouldn't I?" She looked at him, her hand on her hip.

"Probably." He nodded toward Sophia. "But should she?"

Hadley scooped Sophia up into her arms and crossed over to the desk, settling the child once again into the chair. She plucked the child's tablet, encased in a purple protective sleeve, out of her backpack and put it in front of her, along with a juice box. "Okay, sweetie, sit here and watch this cartoon while I talk to Mr. Ryan. Okay?" she said before putting the child's headphones over her ears.

"Yes, Mommy." Sophia nodded, her eyes transfixed on the show in front of her as she slurped her juice.

"Okay." Hadley crossed over and sat on the bed opposite Ryan. "What was this about Parker? Why are you tracking Troy's brother's movements?"

"Linc, I'm putting you on speaker so Hadley can be part of the discussion." Ryan put his phone on speaker mode and placed it on the nightstand. "Troy's brother made some pretty big threats toward me during the trial and after the verdict was read. I don't know that he was the man in the truck, but in order to cross him off the list, I asked Lincoln to monitor Parker's movements."

"Correct," Lincoln interjected. "So I assigned one of our employees to do surveillance at Parker's residence last night. According to his secretary, Parker was in court all day, but it was after midnight before he returned home."

"What does this mean?" Hadley asked.

"It means," Ryan answered, taking off his glasses and rubbing his eyes, "we can't rule him out as the shooter."

"But what about the snowstorm? If he had come all the way to Wyoming, wouldn't the storm have hindered him from getting home?"

"Not necessarily," Linc responded. "The snow started shortly after you ditched the truck following you. If that was Parker, and he knew there was a major storm brewing, he may have continued south, staying ahead of the blizzard instead of sticking around trying to locate you. Also, lying low a few days and giving you a sense of security that you escaped may give him a chance for a surprise attack later."

Shock registered on her face. "I can't believe this. What kind of family did I get mixed up with?" Hadley gasped and clutched her chest. "He took the photo. He knows about Sophia. I can't let them take my daughter. We've got to run, again."

Laughter erupted from the tiny bundle of energy across the room as she watched a cartoon cat chase a mouse around a table, and Ryan knew, without a doubt, that even though he'd met this woman and her child less than twenty-four hours ago, he would do whatever it took to keep them safe. The Odom family could not lay claim to that sweet, innocent child. No matter what.

"Yay, Nonna's House!" Sophia squealed from the back seat.

Although Hadley's heart broke knowing that her mother wouldn't know who they were, she loved how overjoyed her daughter was any time she got to visit Nonna.

"Does she understand about your mom's illness?" Ryan asked as he pulled into a parking space outside the nursing home.

"Not really, but she didn't know her grandmother before the Alzheimer's, so to her this is just how Nonna is." She offered him a smile. "Thank you for bringing us here. I know you would have preferred we skip the visit today, but it's our last chance to visit before Christmas and Sophia really wanted to give Nonna a gift."

Hadley lifted the bouquet of red roses and

white lilies to her face and inhaled their sweet scent.

Ryan turned off the engine and shifted in his seat to look at her. "You're welcome. But remember, if I sense the slightest bit of danger, we're out of here. Got it? We don't want to put your mom or any of the other residents in danger needlessly."

"Agreed." She unbuckled her seat belt, exited the vehicle and quickly released her daughter from her car seat.

The drawing of two women and a little girl standing in front of a house with Christmas lights that Sophia had made at school earlier in the week was clutched in her daughter's hand. When asked about the drawing, Sophia had said it was a picture of when Nonna was well enough to come live with them, and Hadley had had to fight back tears, knowing that would never happen.

Her heart ached for her daughter, who would never know what it was like to have a normal family with grandparents, and aunts and uncles and cousins. Ryan rounded the vehicle as a single tear slid down her face. She quickly wiped it away, praying he hadn't seen her moment of weakness, squared her shoulders and said, "Okay, baby girl, let's go see Nonna."

"I'm not a baby girl. I'm a big girl. I can tie my shoes, and…" Sophia chattered on about all the big-girl things she could do, but Hadley was struggling to focus on anything but Ryan's hand, which he'd placed on the small of her back as they made their way into the building.

What was it about the bodyguard that made her breath catch and her heart skip a beat any time he touched her or looked at her with his blue eyes?

Not able to trust her judgment in men, and with no desire to expose her daughter to an abusive man like Troy, Hadley hadn't looked at any man twice in the past six years and had turned down all men who'd asked her on a date. Which was another reason her reaction to Ryan didn't make any sense.

Her attraction to the man had to be simply because he was being protective of both her and Sophia. Wasn't there some kind of name for a psychological attraction born out of being in close proximity during a stressful situation? She shook her head in a futile attempt to clear her thoughts. Exhaustion and stress had to be the culprit playing tricks on her emotions. Nothing more. As soon as she had a moment to catch her breath and think, she'd come up with a plan to get her and Sophia to a safe place where she could protect them both herself.

SIX

Leaning against the wall closest to the door of the room, Ryan watched as the woman with white hair and Hadley's smile colored with Sophia. The pair sat at a small table in the sunroom that opened into a walled flower garden, giggling and having fun, while Hadley spoke in hushed tones with a nurse in the hallway.

He had to admit, he'd been pleasantly surprised by the security at the facility. When visitors arrived at the entrance, they had to be buzzed inside by a guard, and once inside, there were security cameras on every hall. When they reached the wing where Hadley's mother's small apartment was located, there was even more security, with an additional door and guard. Hadley had said it was because this section of the building housed the Alzheimer's patients, and the additional arrangements were more about keeping the residents inside so they didn't wander off and get lost.

"Mr. Ryan, do ya wanna see my drawing?" Sophia excitedly waved him over.

Ryan smiled, pushed away from the wall and crossed over to the pair. "Sure, sweetie. What did you draw?" He knelt beside the little girl's chair.

Sophia pushed the paper toward him, a smile on her face. Was it a pineapple person with two smaller pineapple people in front of a forest fire? That couldn't be right. He squinted his eyes. "That's a really good…drawing. It's…colorful."

"Do you know what it is?" She got off her chair and stood beside him.

"Um…sure. It's…"

"What a pretty drawing, Sophia," Hadley exclaimed, leaning over Ryan's shoulder.

How had he let her sneak up on him? *Get it together, Vincent. Now is not the time to let your guard down.*

Hadley took the drawing out of his hand and examined it. "That's a really pretty Christmas tree."

The little girl beamed at her mother's praise.

"And I see me and you, but who's the bigger person, here?" Hadley pointed at the biggest pineapple person.

Sophia huffed. "Mr. Ryan, of course."

"Oh, of course. I see it now." Hadley poked Ryan. "Don't you think it's a very good likeness of you?"

He smiled and nodded, unable to get words past the lump in his throat. He'd never had a child draw a picture of him. He gave Sophia an awkward hug and managed a simple "Thank you."

"Sophia's mom, I want you to look at my drawing, too." Hadley's mother held up a wrinkled piece of paper, an eager look on her face.

"I'd be happy to, Nonna." Hadley crossed over to her mother, a tender expression on her face. And accepted the drawing the older woman held out to her. "This is beautiful. Can you tell me who these people are?" She laid the paper down in front of her mother.

The elderly woman reached out a shaky finger and pointed at one of the people in the drawing. "This is my mommy. See her beautiful red hair. And this is my daddy," she added, a frown on her face. "He is gone. He has to work, and I don't get to see him. Most of the time it's just Mommy and me. But Daddy will be home for Christmas. He promised me a new baby doll." She looked around the room. "Where is my mommy? Isn't it time for her to pick me up? I think it's almost time for school to be out, isn't it?"

"No, not yet," Hadley replied.

"I hope it is soon. Mommy said she would make chocolate chip cookies for my afterschool snack." Hadley's mom looked across the table at

Sophia. "Could Sophia come to my house and play?"

"I'm sure she would love that," Hadley answered in a raspy voice that indicated she was fighting back tears. "Right now, Sophia and I have to leave. But we'll try to come back and see you soon."

Ryan scooped Sophia into his arms and stood. Then he smiled at Hadley's mom, wrapped an arm around Hadley's shoulders and guided her toward the door.

"Why is Mommy crying?" Sophia asked, reaching toward her mother and wrapping an arm around her neck. "It's okay, Mommy. I'm here."

"I know, sweetheart." Brushing away the tears and smiling at Ryan, Hadley pulled Sophia into her arms and held her tightly.

They made their way out of the building. "Stay behind me," he instructed, using his arm to gently guide Hadley to walk behind him. "I don't like being out in the open like this, especially since we don't know who we're dealing with."

"So, what's the plan? How do we find out who's after me?"

"We're going to go back to the hotel, then we'll make a list of possible suspects. I'll question you and you might get a little frustrated with me. But oftentimes there are minor details that our brains overlook that someone else can pick up on."

Ryan caught a glimpse of a silver truck driving down a side road, leading to the four-way stop in front of the nursing home. It probably wasn't their attacker, but no point taking chances. He picked up the pace and hurried Hadley and Sophia to his vehicle.

"Fasten her quickly," he demanded. Ryan opened the passenger side door and quickly unlocked the glove compartment so he could retrieve his weapon if needed.

"What is it? What's going on?" Hadley asked frantically as she tightened the car seat straps around Sofia.

He nodded toward the intersection as the truck rolled through the stop sign and turned into the parking lot. "Looks like we have company. Hop in, we've got to go. Now!" He sprinted around the front of his SUV and was already backing out of the parking space as Hadley closed her door.

"I know we can't let them catch us, but remember my daughter is in this vehicle. Don't wreck," she ordered as she snapped her seat belt into place.

Ryan gunned the motor and zoomed out of the parking lot, the silver truck right behind him. Pressing the call button on the steering wheel, he gave the command to call 911. A *call failed* message flashed on the display on the dashboard. The storm from the night before must have interfered with the call towers. He took a deep breath and puffed it out. *Lord, please guide me. I have to keep this mother and daughter safe. I can't let them or Jessica down now.*

Going in the opposite direction of the hotel, he turned left, and a little red car almost sideswiped them. The driver honked at him and threw up her hands, her mouth moving as she obviously gave him a piece of her mind.

"Sorry. So, sorry," he said, even though he knew she couldn't hear him.

"I thought Parker was back in Denver. How'd he get here so fast?" Hadley demanded.

"Either the person after you isn't Parker, or he has someone working with him." Pressing down on the accelerator, Ryan headed away from the main section of town.

"Whee! Go faster, Mr. Ryan," Sophia squealed from the back seat.

"Don't you dare," her mother muttered under her breath so only he could hear. Twisting in her seat, she reached back and handed the ever-present purple tablet to the child. "Here, Sophia, watch a cartoon."

"No, Mommy." Sophia kicked her feet.

Ryan touched Hadley's arm. "Try and call

nine-one-one. Maybe a different cell provider will have service when mine doesn't."

She nodded, settled back into her seat correctly and pulled her phone out of her bag. A few moments later she sighed. "No service."

The silver truck slammed into his back bumper and sent Ryan's SUV skidding over the road. He tightened his grip on the steering wheel and fought to regain control of his vehicle. A minivan topped the next hill and headed straight for them.

"What are we going to do?" Hadley gripped the dashboard.

Ryan sped up and forced his way back into the right lane, clipping the silver truck's front fender. At the same time, the driver of the minivan swerved, hitting a patch of ice and spinning out of control. The minivan straightened but wasn't able to get fully back into the other lane before brushing past Ryan. The sound of metal scraping against metal reverberated inside the vehicle.

"We need to go someplace where we can lose the truck before he causes us to crash with another vehicle. How well do you know this area?"

"Not very. I mainly visit the nursing home… but sometimes I go to the mall. Do you think we could lose him there?"

"I don't know if I like the idea of getting trapped indoors."

"There are multiple exits on the ground floor. And given that it is three days before Christmas, I'm sure it will be very crowded, making it easy for us to get lost."

"I don't like it, but it seems to be our only option. Give me directions."

A few minutes later they pulled into a crowded parking area. Immediately, he realized his mistake. There were no parking spaces, and shoppers walked in and out of traffic, seemingly oblivious to drivers trying to make their way up and down the aisles.

"This is a nightmare," Hadley gasped. "I'm so sorry."

"It's okay." He glanced at her as an idea struck. "We'll get out of this. But you're going to have to trust me."

She nodded and glanced back at the truck that was so close to his bumper no one could walk between them if they tried. "Okay, anything."

Ryan's heart pounded in his chest. He prayed his plan would work. The driver behind him wore sunglasses and a cap pulled low over his face, making it impossible to identify him; however, it was also clear the driver was alone. Which would hopefully give them an advantage.

"Quickly, tell me the layout of this place. Is there parking on all sides of the building and are there other roads out of here?"

"Yes." She gave him a rundown of the other roads surrounding the area. "If you go straight, there's a road that leads to the movie theater that's located at the back of the retail stores." She glanced at him nervously. "Do you have a plan?"

"I do, but you're not going to like it."

She glared at him as if to say, *Out with it already*.

"I need you to unbuckle and lean into the back seat. Get Sophia's panda bear and wrap it in the blanket. Then bring it into the front seat with you, making it look like you've just taken Sophia out of her car seat and are holding her in your lap."

She looked at him a moment, an eyebrow arched, but then did as he instructed. Ryan could only hope the tinted windows on his vehicle would be enough to disguise that it was a stuffed toy and not the child. Without knowing who the person was after, Hadley or Sophia, it had to look like they were both running. It would all come down to Hadley's speed and determination and the gullibility of the person following them. *Please, Lord, let this work.*

She wasn't sure what the plan was, but Hadley knew she had to trust Ryan to get her and her daughter to safety. Without a vehicle of her own, she had no other choice. Glancing out the back window, she made sure the person in the truck was observing her. And even though she couldn't see his eyes because of the sunglasses, the scowl on his face was one of obvious contempt. A shiver ran up her spine, and she hoisted the bear wrapped in the blanket over the seat, settling it into her lap as if it really were Sophia.

"Okay, now what?"

"When I say *go*, you're going to jump out and run."

"What? Are you serious?"

"Look, this is our only chance. We're trapped by all these vehicles and pedestrians. He's stuck behind me. And if he does like I think he will and tries to abandon his vehicle to chase after you, the mall security officer standing on the sidewalk will stop him. Stay in big crowds and work your way to the back of the mall. I'll pick you up at the movie theater."

"You expect me to leave my child in this vehicle and just pray that you're able to get away from the man chasing us if he decides to go after you instead of me?"

"But he's not after me. He's after you." He reached over and squeezed her hand. "Trust me. I won't let anything happen to Sophia."

His eyes pleaded with her, and she found herself caving. Words would not form in her throat, so she nodded. "Okay, the movie theater. Do you think he's going to pursue me?"

"I don't know. The question is, if he does, can you outrun him?"

Thankfully, she was wearing jeans and running shoes instead of the festive dress she'd originally planned to wear to visit her mother today. Running for their lives last night had made the idea of Christmas photos with Nonna go out of her mind when she packed their bags.

She nodded. "Yes."

"Good girl. Okay, unfasten your seat belt and when I start to turn down the next aisle, jump out and run. Don't look back."

Her heart pounded in her ears and her chest tightened, making it difficult to breathe. "Wait. Just a moment, please. I have to tell Sophia goodbye so she doesn't panic." Raising her voice so her daughter could hear her, she said, "Sophia, honey, Mommy is going to get out and run into a store. You're going to stay with Mr. Ryan. Okay?"

"Mommy, I want to go."

Fighting back tears and trying to keep the fear out of her voice, Hadley replied, "Sweetie, there are a lot of people here today. It'll be faster if Mommy goes by herself. Can you be a big girl for Mr. Ryan?"

"Yes, Mommy," Sophia replied, and made a sucking sound.

Sophia was sucking her thumb. A wave of sadness settled over Hadley. She had worked really hard to get Sophia to stop the thumb-sucking habit, but when her daughter felt insecure, she still reverted to it instinctively. Hadley forced herself not to turn and look back, knowing if she did so the driver of the truck would see it and realize that Sophia was not being held in her lap.

Hadley could hear her mother loud and clear. *Choose your battles. This one isn't worth fighting at the moment.* She sighed. They could work on stopping the thumb-sucking again, once this ordeal was over.

"Okay, I'm ready."

"Run like your life depends on it, and don't look back. Got it?"

She laughed. "Running like my life depends on it shouldn't be too difficult. Because it does... Just promise me, no matter what, you'll get Sophia to safety."

He glanced at her, pressed his lips together and nodded.

"There's a small opening in the crowd up ahead. I'm going to try and push my way through before the next group starts across the crosswalk. Hopefully, they'll be able to trap our guy long enough for you to get out and run, providing you with a good head start... Okay... On three... One...two...thr—"

She pushed open the door and darted out of the vehicle before he finished the word. Gripping the panda tightly as she would her child, she pushed her way through the crowd. Car horns blew, followed by slamming doors and lots of yelling, but she pushed on, refusing to look backward. Go, go, go, her mind kept commanding, over and over.

Footsteps pounded behind her and the urge to look over her shoulder was too strong. She glanced back and saw the silver truck blocking traffic and the man coming after her, fighting to push his way through the crowd. Other motorists exited their vehicles, yelling at the man to get back into his vehicle and move it out of the way.

Hadley ducked into a clothing store and peered through the front windows. The crowd had completely surrounded the man, and the mall security officer was headed toward the disturbance. She quickly grabbed a hooded sweatshirt off a shelf and paid the clerk, requesting an extra-large bag so she could shove the panda bear and her coat into it.

Taking a deep breath, she glanced one more time in the direction of the parking lot. The man was begrudgingly getting back into his truck while the officer glared at him. There was no sign of Ryan's vehicle. Hopefully, he'd been able to get out of the overcrowded area and was waiting for her near the movie theater.

A large group of women was exiting the store.

She listened as they talked about heading to a restaurant in the food court area for lunch. Smiling at them, she walked out of the store as if she were part of their group. This time, she didn't look back. If the man wanted to follow her now, he'd have to park first and that would give her the needed time to disappear.

If only she could shake Ryan off just as easily. Now, where had that thought come from? Sure, she had wanted to ditch the security specialist yesterday, but deep down, she knew there was no way she would have made it this far without him. And as much as she hated to admit it, until they knew for sure who was after her, she needed his protection.

SEVEN

Drumming his fingers on the steering wheel, Ryan searched the crowd outside the movie theater for Hadley. Where was she? He'd parked at the curb so she'd be able to spot him. Had the man in the truck nabbed her? Frustration and helplessness washed over him. What had he been thinking? He never should have sent her out on her own.

"Where's Mommy?" Sophia asked for the tenth time.

He turned to look at the child. She had the thumb of one hand in her mouth while a finger on her free hand twirled her hair. Ryan could only imagine how frightened she had to be. "She'll be here soon. I promise. Then Uncle Ryan will buy you a treat. How about that?"

"Are you my uncle?" the little girl asked in awe.

Now, why had he said that? *Can't take it back now.* "No, but—"

A small man in a hooded sweatshirt that

showed a snowman decked out for the holidays on the front was running across the parking lot, headed straight toward them. He reached into the glove compartment, his hand hovering over his gun as the figure reached for the passenger-side door handle.

"Open the door. Let me in!" the person demanded, banging on the window, face pressed against the glass.

"Hadley?"

"Mommy!"

Ryan and Sophia spoke in unison.

Pressing the unlock button, he shifted into Drive.

She dove into the front seat, threw the big shopping bag into the back seat and yelled, "Go, go, go!"

He didn't need to be told twice. Thankfully, the theater area wasn't as crowded and he was able to exit the parking lot in record time. "What happened? And where did you get the…um…interesting sweatshirt?"

Hadley took a few deep breaths. "The guy got out of his truck…tried to follow me…" She panted. "It was…chaos."

"Did he see where you went?" Ryan searched the vehicles in his rearview mirror but didn't see any sign of the truck.

"I don't think so." Her breathing had returned

to normal. "The crowd surrounded him when he got out of his vehicle. Then the mall security officer showed up—like you predicted—and made him move his truck."

"I saw the crowd but got out of there before the officer made it to the guy." Ryan threw on his blinker and made a right turn. "When the people milled around the guy, I got a clear opening to get out of there, because everyone stopped to stare. No one was crossing the road. So, what happened next?"

"I went inside a clothing store. That's where I got this." She motioned to the gawdy Christmas sweatshirt. "I was trying to blend in with the crowd." Turning to the back seat, she pulled the panda bear from the bag.

"Mr. Bamboo," Sophia cried, holding her hands out for her beloved stuffed animal.

For some unknown reason, pride welled inside him. "You did good. I don't think I could've done better."

"Well, I just hope I don't ever have to do that again. It was scary, and I don't ever want to be separated from Sophia in a situation like that again, either." Hadley settled back in her seat and looked at him. "I don't mean to sound ungrateful. Thank you for protecting her."

"You didn't sound ungrateful, you sounded like a mom." He offered her what he hoped was a reassuring smile. He needed to have her trust, because he didn't want her to fight him about going into hiding. Today's attack had simply reinforced what he already knew: they weren't safe out in the open. "I sent Linc a text. We're going to grab our things from the hotel and move to a safer location."

"We have no reason to think the guy knows where we're staying, do we?"

"No, but with our rooms being so far apart, I can't guarantee your safety if he does. After everything you've been through the past six years, are you willing to take the chance with Sophia's life?"

She gasped. He hated how harsh he'd sounded, but he needed to make her realize that she was putting her life and the life of her child in danger by not letting him do his job.

"I'm sorry. I know the answer to that question." He pushed a hand through his hair. "But I'm not sure how to get you to understand the danger."

"I do understand. I'm not trying to fight you, it's just that my mom…" Her voice cracked and she went silent.

His phone buzzed and Linc's name flashed on the screen. Ryan pressed the answer button on the steering wheel. "Hey, Linc. Were you able to find anything close by?"

"Yes. I think you're going to like this." The sound of papers rustling came across the line. "I found a cabin close to the Hogadon Basin ski area. It will be off the beaten path and, I hope, an unlikely place for someone to look for you."

"That's perfect." Ryan looked at Hadley and added, "It keeps us close enough to Hadley's mom that we can get to the nursing home in a hurry if needed."

Hadley's face softened and she rewarded him with a smile. He had no clue how he was going to work things out so she could stay connected to her mom while in hiding, but he would make it happen. He had to. She'd lost so much already because of Troy, and he wouldn't be responsible for adding to her stress.

The roads leading to the ski resort had been cleared by snowplows. Snowbanks lined the road and tall pine trees with their branches bent under the load of the snow covering them stood proudly.

The entire scene reminded Hadley of something straight out of a Christmas movie. The only thing missing was a horse-drawn carriage, a warm red plaid blanket and a thermos of hot chocolate. *And of course, not being on the run for your life.*

"The road to the cabin should be the next left," Ryan said, breaking the silence.

"I'm glad Linc was able to get us a safe place to stay, but do you think this may be too remote?" She tried to keep the fear out of her voice. "There's a prediction of more snow tonight. What if we get trapped here?"

"As my aunt Lydia would say, there's no point begging for trouble."

"And that means…?"

"Don't worry about something before it happens." He put on his blinker and slowed to turn into the drive leading to what he hoped would be their safe haven. "We bought enough food to last for days. Worst-case scenario, we'll be well fed, warm and sheltered."

"No, worst-case scenario, we'll be trapped and easy prey for a—" she lowered her voice in a whisper "—killer."

"He'll have to find us first. And I promise, I've kept an eye on all the vehicles we've encountered on the drive from the motel to the cabin. There's not been any sign of the silver truck."

She knew his words were meant to ease her anxious mind, but she couldn't help but feel like there was something he wasn't telling her. *How much do I really know about this man I'm trusting to keep me and Sophia safe? Honestly, not enough.*

She was beginning to regret not having her own vehicle. There wasn't anything she could do about that now, but she wouldn't hesitate to take Ryan's SUV and run if need be.

"Here we are, home sweet *temporary* home," Ryan declared, pulling her out of her thoughts.

The cabin looked more like a small shack from the outside. Hopefully, it was a little nicer inside. Stepping out of the vehicle, she could see that someone had hung an evergreen wreath with a red ribbon on the door and there were white lights strung under the porch eaves. Maybe it wouldn't be so bad after all.

Hadley released Sophia from her car seat and settled her on the ground.

"Where are we, Mommy?" Sophia asked as she looked around in awe.

"We're at a cabin in the forest," Hadley said, trying to make her voice light and happy. "We're going to have a fun adventure."

Please, Lord, let Sophia remain in the dark about what's really happening here. Let her continue to think the fast driving and running is a game. Protect her innocence.

"A little help here, please," Ryan pleaded as he tried to punch the code into the lockbox to retrieve the key to the front door, his arms full of grocery bags.

Sophia giggled. "I can't help. I too young."

"You, young lady, may carry Mr. Bamboo and your backpack." She slipped the pack onto her daughter's tiny shoulders. "Now let's help Mr. Ryan open the cabin door."

"Um... 'kay, we're coming, Uncle Ryan."

Uncle Ryan? What had brought that on? Hadley would have to address the issue soon, laying out clear boundaries for both her daughter and *Uncle Ryan*. She couldn't have Sophia getting attached to Ryan Vincent. For one thing, he'd be leaving soon to go back to Colorado and she didn't want Sophia to be crushed when that happened. And for another, the man had most likely brought the danger to their doorstep.

"That's everything." Ryan dropped his overnight bag on the floor beside the fireplace and crossed over to the small kitchen island, where Sophia sat eating apple slices. Hadley was preparing grilled cheese sandwiches to go along with the tomato soup that bubbled in the saucepan. "I put your suitcase and Sophia's backpack in the bedroom. There's a queen-size bed, so you gals should be comfortable."

"What about you?" Hadley pointed with the spatula. "That couch doesn't look very comfortable. I feel guilty that you're stuck here with us and don't even have a decent place to lay your head."

"Don't. I've slept in worse places. Remember, I was a marine." He could tell horror stories about some of the places where he'd had to try and catch a catnap, but he'd spare her the gory details. "So, what time does the munchkin go to sleep? You and I really need to sit down and make a list of suspects."

"What's sus-ects mean?" Sophia looked at him questioningly.

Ryan looked at Hadley for assistance, but she simply smiled and raised an eyebrow. She was obviously enjoying his discomfort. He settled onto the vacant barstool beside the little girl. How did one answer all the questions of a five-year-old? With honesty. Well, to a degree anyway. "It's another word for people."

"Then why didn't you say *people*?"

Hadley giggled and used the spatula to lift the corner of the grilled cheese to test for doneness.

"I don't know, squirt. I guess, maybe, sometimes adults try to make things more difficult than they have to be."

Sophia climbed onto his lap, her arm around his neck as she searched his face. "Is that why you call me all those strange names?"

"What strange names?"

"You called me munch-kim. And squirt." She huffed. "My name is So-phi-a. It's not hard to say."

Hadley burst out laughing, not even trying to hide her amusement any longer, while Ryan stared aghast at the child on his lap who may technically still be a preschooler but acted like she was five going on thirty-five. He recalled a similar conversation with Bridget when she confronted him about calling her a variety of nicknames. Though he'd meant them as terms of endearment, in both cases, it seemed they could come across negatively. Ryan would have to do better with the women in his life.

"I'm sorry, Sophia. I like nicknames, but I'll try and do better."

"What does nicknames mean?" She tilted her head and waited for an answer.

"Well, it's a special name you call someone you care about. One—"

"Okay, time to eat," Hadley interrupted his explication, putting a small bowl of soup and a saucer with two triangle-shaped pieces of sandwich in front of Sophia. "Then it's off to bed for you, young lady."

Ryan eased the child out of his lap and back onto her seat.

"Okay, Mommy. But I want Uncle Ryan to read me a story," Sophia declared through a mouth full of cheese sandwich.

The child's declaration tugged at his heartstrings. His sister Bridget had been five years old when he'd been adopted by their parents, and she'd been just like sweet Sophia. Full of questions, fierce and fragile all at the same time. *Watch it, Vincent. Don't let your emotions get involved. Once you capture the person intent on harming this family, you'll be leaving and out of their lives forever. Just like the goal was in the Marines. Go in, do your job, and leave without a trace.*

He met Hadley's gaze above the little girl's head. She shrugged and turned back to the stove to finish serving up the meal.

Forty-five minutes and two bedtime stories later, Sophia was finally asleep. Ryan walked out of the bedroom, closing the door gently behind him. He entered the living room to find that Hadley had cleaned the kitchen and was sitting on the sofa with a notepad in her lap and a pen in her hand.

"What are you working on?"

She tapped her pen on the notepad. "Thought I'd get a head start on that list."

"Good. What have you gotten so far?" He plopped down on the couch and held out his hand.

Hadley handed him the notepad. "Nothing. The only name that comes to mind is Troy. If he's in prison, it can't be him. And I know you mentioned Parker, but logically, why would he be after me? I didn't have anything to do with Troy going to prison, so he can't be mad at me about that." Her voice cracked, and she looked up at him, tears shimmering in her eyes. "Who wants me dead? And what will happen to Sophia if they succeed?"

"Hey, now, don't talk like that. I'm not going to let anything happen to you or Sophia, got it?"

"I know you mean well, and I know you sincerely think you can protect us. But sometimes things don't go as planned." The tears flowed freely now.

Ryan had to fight the urge to sweep her up into his arms and soothe her as she cried silently in front of him. He knew she was thinking about Jessica, and as much as he had wanted to blame Hadley for his fiancée's death after he discovered what they'd done, he knew it wasn't Hadley's fault. And while he'd never understand why Jessica had let Troy into her home that night, it wasn't her fault, either. The only person responsible was Troy. And he'd spend the rest of his life in prison paying for his actions.

She wiped her tears and took a deep breath releasing it slowly. "Do you really think it could be Parker after me? I never did anything to him. Actually, I only ever met him once, and that was almost seven years ago."

He took off his glasses and pinched the bridge of his nose. "I honestly don't know. If he is behind it, he has to have hired someone to do the dirty work for him. Remember, Linc said Parker arrived home late last night. There's no way he was the person in the truck after us earlier."

"You're right! I had forgotten that." She took the notepad out of his hand and stared at it. "I have no clue who is after me. How do I fight the unknown?"

Her look of complete helplessness was his undoing. He scooted closer, wrapped his arm around her and pulled her close. "This isn't the same as the last time you were running from danger. This time, you're not alone. And I'm not going to leave your side until we know exactly who's after you and we've stopped them."

He kissed the top of her head like he had his sister's many times through the years, soothing her heartaches. Only, this wasn't his sister, and he needed to remind himself of that, multiple times a day if necessary, to keep himself from becoming too attached to her. Because whether or not, Hadley was responsible for Jessica's death, if Hadley hadn't involved her in her life and drama, Jessica would be alive. They'd be married and possibly have a child of their own by now. And he'd be at home preparing to celebrate Christmas with his family. Instead, he was on the run with his fiancée's murderer's daughter and ex-girlfriend while trying to keep them from being killed.

EIGHT

Folding the lumpy bed back into the sofa, Ryan quickly put the cushions back into place. Then he crossed over to the kitchen and made himself a cup of coffee, his third since he'd woken an hour ago. 6:36 a.m. The clock on the stove flashed the time tauntingly. It had been a long night. He hadn't fallen asleep until almost midnight, and then he'd tossed and turned, hearing every nature sound throughout the night before giving up on the idea of resting.

His eyes fell on the notepad on which Hadley had finally written three or four names last night. Pulling out his cell phone, he snapped a photo of the list of names and sent the image in a text to Lincoln, along with instructions to see what he could find out about the people and their past to see if any of them had a criminal record.

After pulling on his hiking boots, he shrugged into his heavy winter jacket and gloves and headed outdoors to explore the area closest to the cabin. When he returned, he would prepare breakfast for the girls and then dig out his laptop to do his own research on the people in Hadley's life. Ninety percent of the time, attackers were people the victim knew or had a relationship with. Hadley hadn't included any men she'd dated on the list. Why had the thought that she hadn't dated since moving to Wyoming make him happy? He shook his head. Ryan would have to probe her on her dating life this evening and see if any names needed to be added to their very small list of suspects. No, acquaintances. Hadley had insisted they weren't suspects, at least not until he could prove otherwise.

Ryan stepped onto the small wooden porch that housed a lone rocking chair. He imagined it would be a nice place to sit and relax with a cup of coffee and watch the sunrise, on a warmer day, anyway. The early-morning quietness enveloped him. Where were the critters that had kept him awake all night with their chatter? Probably resting so they could keep him awake again tonight.

His phone dinged, alerting him to a new text message. Linc had sent a thumbs-up emoji, acknowledging the text Ryan had sent earlier. As usual, his partner was up early. Most likely he was already at the office, as it was his custom to be the first to arrive and the last to leave. Now that Ryan had successfully captured Troy, and he was behind bars where he couldn't hurt anyone else, Ryan hoped to be a better business partner and pull more of his weight in the office. Lincoln had carried the load too long and deserved a vacation.

Ryan canvassed the area quickly. Nothing unusual jumped out at him. Guess the noises in the night had been exactly as he had thought. The sound of a snowplow drew closer and he could see it in the distance through the trees. They must be clearing the main roads for the day's visitors.

Too bad the snowplows couldn't clear the driveway to the cabins. Not wanting the snow to become too deep and block their exit, Ryan grabbed the snow shovel he'd seen leaning against the corner of the cabin when they arrived and got to work. Almost an hour later, he put the snow shovel back where he'd found it and wiped his sweat-drenched brow. Time to head indoors and warm up.

In an effort to knock the snow off his shoes, he gently bumped his feet against the edges of the porch steps as he climbed them. One step from the top, he froze and listened. Giggles and laughter filled the air. He smiled and his heart swelled. Sophie and Hadley were awake.

As he opened the front door, the aroma of bacon and eggs wafted to him, and his stomach growled.

"Good morning, Uncle Ryan!" Sophia tackled his legs with a bear hug.

He ruffled her hair. "Good morning, Sophia. Did you sleep well?"

"Uh-huh." She nodded and ran back to the couch, where a cartoon movie played on her purple tablet.

"You didn't have to cook," Ryan said, crossing to the kitchen and standing at the island. "I had planned to make breakfast. I don't want you to think that you have to prepare every meal and do the cleanup. I'll do my share."

She smiled at him over her shoulder. "I think you've been doing your share. I wasn't out there helping you shovel snow and that's no small task. Let's not worry about who does what. We will each do what we can. Now go get cleaned up. Breakfast is almost ready."

"Yes, ma'am." Ryan hurried down the hall to the only restroom. He emerged five minutes later with a clean-shaven face and clean hands and headed back to the kitchen, pausing when he saw Hadley and Sophia seated at the table, their heads bowed in prayer.

Dear Lord, what lesson am I supposed to learn from this family?

* * *

"I'm telling you, I don't have a single coworker who would want to hurt me." Hadley dropped the notepad and pen onto the table, frustration evident on her face. "And besides my coworkers and Sophia's daycare teacher, the bag boy and cashier at the local Food Mart, there is no one else that I interact with on a daily basis."

Ryan knew she was a religious person; he'd seen the many prayers she and Sophia shared. "What about church? Do you and Sophia attend regularly and who are the people you interact with there?"

"Do you really think someone from church could be behind something so evil?"

He sighed. "In an ideal world, the answer would be no. But we don't live in a perfect world. Evil lurks everywhere."

Hadley frowned at Ryan and shook her head, and then she stood and walked over to the sofa where Sophia sat watching a cartoon on her tablet. "Okay, sweetie, time's up."

The little girl whimpered when Hadley took the tablet out of her hands. "But, Mommy."

"No arguing. You've been allowed extra device time the past couple of days because we've been…traveling…but we're back on schedule now." Hadley picked up the stuffed panda off the floor and handed the cherished toy to Sophia.

"Take Mr. Bamboo and go into the bedroom and color. I left the coloring book and crayons on the nightstand."

"Yes, Mommy," Sophia said, doing as instructed.

Once the little girl was gone, Hadley returned to her seat at the dining table. "You may continue your questioning, now that little ears are out of the room."

What had he said that was inappropriate around Sophia? *Evil lurks everywhere?* That was simply the truth. And Ryan thought it was important for kids to grow up knowing this. But Sophia wasn't his kid. Her kid, her rules.

"Look, I know this is difficult and you don't want to believe anyone in your group of friends and acquaintances could do something so horrific as to target you and Sophia. But if I am to keep you safe, I have to know all aspects of your life."

"Does this mean you've ruled out Parker?"

He took off his glasses and rubbed his temples. Ryan wished he had thought to purchase some headache medicine at the grocery store yesterday. Maybe more caffeine would help. Pushing away from the table, he crossed to the coffeepot and refilled his cup.

"No. Parker is still on the list, but if he's responsible, he's hired someone to do the dirty work. Most likely, it's someone from the area, and could be someone you know."

"Okay, I get it. I will try—" Her phone dinged, indicating she'd received a text message, and the name Carlton flashed on the screen.

"Who is Carlton?" he demanded as she read the message. "Why haven't you mentioned him?"

A smile lifted the corner of her lips. "He's a sweet, elderly man who I met at the nursing home four months ago, when he was there for rehab following hip replacement surgery."

"Why is he texting?"

She held out her phone for him to read the message himself.

Don't forget Sophia's riding lesson this afternoon at 3:00.

"Riding lesson?"

"Uh-huh." She nodded as she typed a response. "Carlton owns one of the largest cattle ranches in the area. Misty Hollow Ranch. After meeting Sophia, he insisted she needed to learn to ride horses and has graciously allowed her to take lessons at his ranch."

"You are telling him you won't make it, right?"

"Of course, I am. I don't want to lead danger to Carlton."

"So you're telling him…"

"Sophia and I had to go out of town unexpectedly, but I'll let him know when we return so we can resume the riding lessons."

"Great. Now tell me everything you can about Carlton, beginning with his last name." How was he going to make her understand that her life and her daughter's life depended on her being completely honest with him and not keeping secrets. Even details that she felt were minor needed to be shared.

Hadley didn't understand why Ryan was so upset. She had been completely honest with him. With everything that had happened, she just hadn't thought about Carlton or Sophia's riding lessons. She hadn't been trying to keep secrets. "Carlton McIntyre, age seventy-eight. One child. A daughter named Mikael. Numerous employees, including a housekeeper, a cook, a ranch foreman and—"

"Whoa." Ryan held up his hands in surrender. "Look, I get it. You're annoyed that I questioned why you hadn't mentioned Carlton. I'm sorry if I offended you. I'm not suggesting your friend is involved, but we do need a thorough list of all the people you've crossed paths with the past few months. Why don't we start by making a list of the people you've interacted with at McIntyre's ranch?"

Hadley had written three names on the page when her phone rang. Carlton's name flashed on the screen. She raised an eyebrow and looked at Ryan.

He shrugged, then nodded for her to answer the call. "Put it on speaker."

She bit back her annoyance that he would feel the need to eavesdrop on her conversation and did as he instructed. "Hi, Carlton."

"Hadley, are you and Sophia all right?"

"We're fine. We just needed a little vacation."

"Don't try and fool me." He huffed. "I heard about your intruder. Sheriff Ramsey said your house was ransacked and that someone shot at you. Now, who would do a thing like that?"

"We're…"

Ryan touched her arm and shook his head. He wrote something on the notepad and slid it toward her. *Keep the details vague.* She nodded.

"I'm sure it was just a random break-in."

"Random break-ins aren't generally followed by a drive-by shooting, young lady." Carlton's tone was harsher than she'd ever heard.

"I'm sure it was because I startled the burglar, and he was afraid I could identify him."

"Well, can you?"

"No. Everything happened too quickly."

Why did she suddenly feel as if she were being interrogated? "Listen, Carlton, I appreciate your concern, but I need to go. I'll call you after the holidays and arrange for Sophia to have her next riding lesson."

"Promise me one thing. You'll call me if you and Sophia need anything. Please."

"I promise. But don't worry about us. We will be fine. We're not alo—"

Ryan put a finger to his lips and shook his head.

"Carlton, I need to go. We'll talk soon." She disconnected the call.

"Thank you. I know it's hard not to disclose details to those close to you, but right now, I really believe it's best."

"You're right. I'm sorry." She rubbed the back of her neck. The feeling of walking on eggshells was starting to play on her nerves. If they didn't catch the person after them soon, she didn't know what she would do. One thing was for sure, she was wasn't cut out for hiding out and being secretive. Six years ago, it had been just her, at least once she got her mother settled into the new nursing home. And while she had been extra cautious and tried to cover her tracks, she hadn't had anyone watching her every move or second-guessing her choices.

Of course, if she were being honest with herself, it had been nice having someone else come up with the plan of escape yesterday. And even though she hadn't liked leaving Sophia behind, it had worked perfectly. It was nice not having to go through this alone. She could easily get used to having Ryan around. *Lord, help me remember Ryan's help is only temporary. I will be on my own again once the person targeting me is caught.*

NINE

What was taking Hadley and Sophia so long in the restroom? Ryan moved to the back wall of the outfitters store and examined the backpack toddler carriers. Weight limit forty-five pounds. He doubted Sophia weighed that much since she was very petite. He selected a moss green one and carried it to the counter, where the clerk already held two sets of snowshoes and a few other supplies Ryan had gathered.

"I'll take this, too. And I think that's all I need today," he said to the gangly teenage clerk. "If you'll ring it up, I'll be right back to pay."

"Yes, sir."

The bell over the door rang, and four college-age women entered the store, followed by a dark-haired man with his cowboy hat pulled low over his eyes. Ryan made a beeline to the restroom in the far corner of the store. The store was small, and it only had two single-occupant restrooms, one for men and one for women.

Knocking on the door of the women's restroom, he whispered, "Everything okay in there?"

"Be right out," Hadley replied. The sound of a hand dryer followed, and then the door opened. "Sorry. It takes time to get Sophia all fastened up in her snow gear."

The little girl was covered head to toe in a purple snowsuit, the hood pulled tightly over her head and a scarf around her face. The only part showing was her hazel eyes, so like her mother's.

Ryan leaned close to Hadley's ear. "The store is getting crowded. Take the keys. Go straight to the vehicle. And lock yourselves in."

She nodded and fisted her hand around the keys he'd slipped into them. They walked back to the front of the store, him stopping at the checkout and the mother and daughter going out the door.

A few moments later, he had stashed the supplies into the back of his SUV and was pulling out of the parking lot.

Hadley sat sideways in her seat, and he felt her eyes boring into him. "You sure bought a lot of stuff. Do you really think we're going to need snowshoes, freeze-dried meals and solar blankets?"

"I hope not, but I'd rather be prepared and not need the items than need them and not have them at my disposal." He pulled to a stop at a four-way stop, and a truck came to a stop behind him. It looked like the vehicle that had followed them yesterday, but he couldn't be sure. The driver seemed a little shorter than the other guy, and this time there were two people in the vehicle, though he couldn't make out the gender of either occupant. Just to be on the safe side, he decided to make a left turn at the last minute.

"What are you doing? That isn't the way back to the cabin."

"I'm trying to make sure that we aren't followed. One can't be too cautious."

She looked over her shoulder and saw the truck. "Is that him?"

"I don't think so, but I can't be sure." He watched in the rearview mirror as the truck went straight at the intersection, not following him. Ryan released a breath. "Guess that's our answer."

"Will I ever reach a point in my life where I don't have to constantly look over my shoulder?"

He reached across and squeezed her hand. "Yes, and I'll make sure of it." Now, why had he made a promise he couldn't keep? *Focus, Vincent. Do your job and go back to Colorado.*

"Mommy, I hungry." Sophia kicked the back of her mother's seat.

"I'll fix you a grilled cheese sandwich when we get back to the cabin."

He leaned over and whispered so only Hadley could hear, "I added a pack of trail mix with nuts, chocolate and peanut butter chips, and assorted dried fruit they had at the counter to our purchase while checking out. If it's okay with you, I don't mind her having some as a snack later."

"You know, they put those items near the checkout so people will make impulse purchases."

"I know." He turned and winked at her. "But at least I picked out a somewhat healthier treat and didn't buy the gummy candy or the sloth keychain that said *Don't hurry, be happy*."

A smile lit her face and her eyes twinkled. "Good job using resistance and avoiding high-pitch sales techniques. And thank you. She will like the special treat."

Later that afternoon, Hadley examined the carrier Ryan had purchased for Sophia. It looked solid enough, and when they tested it out earlier, Sophia had fit inside it, but Hadley still had her doubts about her daughter staying still and quiet if they had to make a run for it. All she could do was pray they wouldn't have to take off through the woods to escape.

"Mommy." Sophia came down the hall dragging Mr. Bamboo behind her. "Can we go home now?"

"Aren't you having fun?"

"I miss my bed and my toys." Sophia pouted as tears welled in her eyes.

Ryan entered the back door and stomped his feet on the mat. "I shoveled the driveway again and pulled the SUV behind the cabin so it can't be seen from the road."

"Won't people driving by know this cabin is occupied, since the drive has been shoveled?"

"Yes. But hopefully they won't know it's us." He moved to the kitchen. "Okay, what would you girls like for dinner?"

"Chicken nuggets." Sophia yelled her favorite meal, bouncing up and down.

"Okay, chicken nuggets and fries it is." Ryan reached into the freezer, pulled out two bags and froze, peering out the window.

"What's—"

He held up a hand to silence her. "Shhh…"

He tossed the frozen bags of food into the sink. "They found us!" he said, rushing across the room and grabbing Sophia. "You remember the game we played this afternoon?"

Her daughter nodded, her unruly hair bobbing as she did so. "Uh-huh. Jungle Run. Gotta be quiet so we don't—" Her words were cut off as Hadley pulled a thick sweater over her head. "Disturb the sleeping bears."

"Okay, sweetheart, the quiet game starts now."

She quickly threaded her daughter's arms and legs through her warm snowsuit and zipped her up as Ryan finished fastening the toddler carrier to his back.

Hadley picked up Sophia and plopped her into the carrier, tightening the straps. Then she grabbed her backpack and coat.

"Remember." He bent and held her gaze. "I will protect Sophia. I promise. If we get separated, keep running. You don't look back. Get to the safe place we found earlier."

Ryan pushed open the back door, and he and Hadley quickly slipped into their snowshoes. The sound of vehicle tires crunching on the drive punctuated the urgency of the situation as they ran into the forest surrounding the cabin, Hadley in the lead, with Ryan following in her path to minimize their tracks. *Lord, protect us.*

Ryan's heart hammered in his chest and flashbacks of tromping through the desert of Afghanistan during his last deployment flashed through his mind. *Fellow marines shot and bleeding. His best buddy among them. Ryan attempting to lift him onto his back so he could carry him to safety, but Pete telling him to leave him. He said he wasn't going to make it and for Ryan to go. Go. Go. Go.* His friend's voice reverberated with every step Ryan took.

The backpack Ryan carried strapped to his chest helped counter the weight of Sophia on his back, keeping him upright, but the combined weight slowed him down. Hadley reached the thicket of trees ahead of him and, despite his warnings to do otherwise, turned to urge them on. He wanted to yell for her to run, but was afraid of being heard.

The silver truck rounded the side of the cabin, the headlights sweeping across the backyard, falling a few feet short of where he stood. Ryan froze beside a big pine tree and prayed Sophia would stay quiet.

The truck doors slammed as two people exited the vehicle, the darkness concealing their identity. "You go around to the front so they can't escape. I'll go in the back," commanded a deep male voice.

The instant the people were out of sight, Ryan ran. He reached Hadley and whispered, "Change of plans. Remember the small cave? That's our new destination."

"What? No. It's too close to the cabin."

"We don't have a choice. The longer we are out in the open the more vulnerable we'll be."

"But—"

"Trust me."

She nodded and took off with him right behind her. A few moments later, he could hear shouting and the cabin door flew open. Uh-oh. They would be after them now. Hopefully, the fact they didn't have snowshoes would slow them down, giving Ryan and Hadley the upper hand.

"Remember, keep moving. Now go." He urged her forward. They rushed through the trees toward the small cave they'd found on their afternoon hike.

Please, Lord, let this new plan work.

They reached the opening of the cave, and Ryan dropped his pack inside. "Help me get Sophia out of the carrier."

Hadley shrugged out of her backpack and then reached for her daughter.

"Mommy, this is a fun game," Sophia squealed.

"Shhh...don't forget we have to be really quiet." Hadley whispered as she pulled Sophia close.

Ryan took off the toddler carrier and threw it into the shallow cave. Then he reached into the pack he had deposited upon arrival and withdrew his gun, tucking it into his waistband. "I'm going to try and lead them away from you."

Hadley grabbed his arm in a vise grip, the fear evident in her eyes even in the waning sunlight. "Don't leave us! What if they find us? I can't protect myself against them out here."

Sophia's eyes widened, her mouth gaping as she looked from her mother to him and back again, obviously becoming aware this was more than a game.

Ryan leaned toward Hadley, his lips brushing her ear as he whispered, "Trust me. It will be okay. I won't let you out of my sight unless I know they are following me."

She nodded agreement, but her face still registered doubt.

It was as if Sophia sensed her mother's distress—tears welled in her eyes, one slipping down her sweet little cheek. He wiped the tear away with his thumb. Then he rested his forehead against Sophia's smaller one. "Trust me. I won't let anything happen to you or your mommy. So be a good girl, okay? And be very quiet, no matter what you hear outside." The child stuck her thumb into her mouth and nodded.

Without stopping to think, he kissed the top of her head, then reached over and kissed Hadley's forehead. "That goes for you, too."

She nodded and ducked into the cave, still holding her daughter tightly.

The sound of the two people in the backyard shouting to go one way or the other reached his ears. He quickly pushed the dried brush he'd casually gathered earlier—when they'd done a run-through of scenarios—into place, praying it hid the opening. Then he headed back in the direction of the cabin.

He topped the small hill leading back to the cabin and froze. The men were headed straight for him.

The sound of a vehicle turning into the driveway caught his and the intruders' attention. Red and blue lights flashed on the house and surrounding woods as a white crew cab truck, with the Natrona County Sheriff logo on the side, pulled to the side of the house. A deputy got out of the vehicle and Ryan ducked behind a tree so he could listen.

"Hey, what's going on here?" The officer walked toward the two men.

The taller intruder yelled something and both men jumped into their truck. The deputy rushed toward them, but they sped off and disappeared around the side of the house. The deputy ran back to his vehicle as he requested assistance over the radio attached at his shoulder, then he hopped into his truck and raced after them.

Ryan sprinted back to the cave, his lungs burning from the exertion. "Hadley…it's…all clear." He pushed the dried limbs out of the way and Hadley and Sophia crawled out from their hiding spot.

"Uncle Ryan. Are the bad men gone?" Sophia dove into his arms, knocking him backward.

"Yes, sweetie. They're gone for now, but we need to hurry."

Hadley pulled the backpacks and toddler carrier out of the cave and pushed to her feet. "Where did they go? What happened? Are you sure we're safe?"

He wanted to tell her he was sure they were safe, but he couldn't. The only thing Ryan was sure of at the moment was that he wished he had backup. But with it being two days before Christmas, he could not ask any of his employees to sacrifice time with their families to travel to Wyoming and protect Hadley and Sophia against an unknown enemy.

"In life there are no guarantees, but we will continue to move around and stay a step ahead of this person. Trust me."

She walked beside him, Sophia in her arms. "You keep saying that. *Trust me*. But for the past six years I've had to learn the only person I could trust was myself."

He hadn't realized that he'd said *Trust me* so many times. Why would he feel the need to re-iterate that he was trustworthy? Those were not words he would normally say to a friend or a client. But Hadley wasn't really either of those things. Although in the past forty-eight hours, he had felt a friendship building with this beautiful woman and her child. No time to analyze his actions or emotions at the moment.

"A sheriff's deputy showed up and the guys

took off. Now hurry, we need to get out of here before they return." He reached for Sophia, pulled her close to his chest and raced toward the cabin.

"Where are we going? Do you have a plan?" Hadley demanded, pushing herself to keep up with his longer strides.

Thankfully, they only had a few hundred feet to go. He made a concentrated effort to slow his stride so it wouldn't be as difficult for her. "Honestly, I don't know. We'll have to come up with a plan after we leave the park. First order of business is to get somewhere out of sight. Then, we may need to look into getting a rental vehicle so they won't know what we're driving. After that..." He swallowed the rest of his words. No need to upset her with the idea of finding someone to take Sophia and keep her safe until he had all of the other things in place.

"After that?" she questioned.

"We'll come up with a plan that keeps you both safe, trust—" He shook his head and increased his stride, the cabin and his SUV in sight.

Where are Bridget and Lincoln when I need them? I know, Lord, I know. They are at home with their families. This is my burden to bear, not theirs. Jessica died to protect this precious soul, and now it's up to me to keep her and her mom alive. He hugged Sophia, and she wrapped her arms tightly around his neck, returning his embrace. A warmth he hadn't felt in a long time seeped into his heart. He could almost physically feel the coldness that had caused him to become a man of action over a man of feeling break away. And while he had never felt like he had turned his back on the Lord, having continued to attend church services and praying and studying on the rare occasions when he actually thought to do so, he suddenly realized he had spoken more to the Lord since entering Hadley and Sophia's lives than he had in five years. For which he needed to be thankful. *Thank You, Lord, for trusting me with this important mission.*

TEN

Hadley watched once again as the trees outside the vehicle sped past the windows while she attempted to squelch the rising fear that threatened to overtake her. What were they going to do? Where could they go this close to the holidays and find a vacancy? She really wished she could suggest going back to her house—she missed the safety she had felt there. Ryan had mentioned the need for a different vehicle. Could they go retrieve her MINI Cooper? No, probably not. The intruder had seen it and would know it was hers.

She racked her brain trying to think of hotels or vacation rental properties within an hour's drive of their location. "What kind of place are we looking for as a hideout?"

"I'm not sure. But I wonder if we were safer at the motel. I cannot imagine how they found us inside the park." He shoved his hand through his dark hair, and a muscle in his jaw twitched.

"Stop. I can tell you're blaming yourself.

Don't. Without you…" Her voice cracked. "Sophia and I wouldn't have made it this far."

"You don't know that." He flashed her a quick smile. "But it never hurts to have a friend who has your back, and I want to be that person."

Her heart quickened. It had been a long time since she'd had a friend she could rely on to be there when she needed someone. Hadley had to remind herself Ryan's presence in her life was only temporary. She and Sophia could not develop deeper feelings for him or come to depend on him. As soon as the person who was after them was captured—or maybe even sooner if it took a long time to find who was tormenting her—Ryan would be gone. It was Christmas. He would want to spend the holiday with his family, and rightfully so.

Maybe it was time for plan B. She took a deep breath and slowly released it. "Would it be possible for Protective Instincts to relocate my mother to another nursing home?"

"Sure. I could make that happen. Do you have a place in mind?"

"No, not really. Just a place with a pond and a pretty view. Mom likes to sit outside." Silent tears streamed down her face. Hadley turned her head to look out the window and scrubbed her palm across her cheeks in a futile attempt to dry them.

Ryan touched her shoulder. "What brought this on? Don't give up on me now."

She shook her head and faced him. "I want my mom to be safe. I have a plan, but it means I won't be around to take care of her."

He pulled back his hand, as if she had suddenly burned him, and slammed it on the steering wheel. "Let's hear this plan," he said, his jaw clenched. "Then I'll decide if I think it's an appropriate course of action. Okay?"

She glanced into the back seat. A smile crept onto her lips. Thankfully, Sophia was sound asleep, Mr. Bamboo tucked under her head as her pillow. Hadley wasn't sure how or why, but riding in the car always seemed to lull her daughter to sleep.

"I developed a plan B years ago, always knowing there would come a time that I might need to run again." She settled back into her seat, tucking one foot under her. "I have passports for Sophia and—"

"No. Absolutely not. Do you expect me to put you and Sophia on a plane to a foreign country?" Ryan sounded horrified at the idea.

"Hear me out. Please."

Silence enveloped the vehicle, and she began to think he was going to ignore her plea.

"Okay. But will you promise to keep an open mind and listen to my take on the situation?"

She nodded. "Of course. But you need to know this is not a whim or a wild, spur-of-the-moment idea. I've spent the past six years developing an exit plan for this situation."

"Actually, your plan was to escape Troy. He's in prison. And he can't hurt you."

"You're right. The plan was in place so I could escape Troy. But isn't this a greater danger, not knowing who the enemy is?" She struggled to tamp down her annoyance. Realistically, she knew Ryan was only wanting to protect her, but spending so many years depending on no one but herself meant that she had to do what she thought was best for her daughter's safety. With or without Ryan's agreement. The best thing to do was to convince him to find a hotel near an airport so she could make her escape if needed. "Maybe you were right and it's time we leave the area. We could head to Cheyenne."

What was she up to? Ryan couldn't believe her sudden interest in going to Cheyenne was simply to find a hotel. "Maybe. Let's get out of the ski area first, then we'll develop a plan. These narrow roads with slow speed limits and a lack of exits make me nervous."

The two-lane road that wound through the area had seemed like a good idea when they'd first arrived. Going slow in a line of vehicles and travel trailers meant no one was likely to sneak up from behind, but now, with the urgency to leave weighing heavy on his shoulders, the drive felt excruciatingly painful.

His phone rang, shattering the silence, and he involuntarily jumped. Lincoln's name flashed on the screen on the dash. He pressed the call button on the steering wheel. "Hello."

"Hey, Ryan. I wanted to let you know, as soon as Bridget and Sawyer get here, we're headed your way."

"What? No. There's no need for you all to sacrifice your holiday with family." He winced inwardly at his own words. Hadley must feel the same way about his presence. No wonder she was trying to make an escape that wouldn't involve him.

"Save your breath. We will always have your back. I may not have understood your need to pursue Troy all these years and not let the police handle it, but I always respected your devotion to my sister and your desire to be the one to capture her killer. And now I want—no, I need—to help you fulfil your final commitment to Jessica and stop whoever is after Hadley and little Sophia, so they can be safe and live a happy life."

His final commitment to Jessica. That might have been how this started, but it had turned to more than an obligation to honor Jessica's memory. He was determined to find out who was behind the attacks and why they were after Hadley, or Sophia. Ryan still wasn't sure who the true target was.

A motor home that had been parked in a small pull-off area nosed its way onto the road between him and the car he'd been following for the past three miles, and he had to put on his brakes. Several vehicles behind him blew their horns, even though he was sure they knew the only thing they accomplished by doing so was blowing off a little steam.

"What's all that noise?" Lincoln asked.

"Just frustrated people blowing their horns because a motor home pulled onto the highway, slowing them down to ten miles per hour versus the fifteen miles per hour they were traveling." Ryan chuckled.

"A motor home. In Wyoming, in the winter? Wait a minute. Why are you in the vehicle?" Linc demanded. "Are Hadley and Sophia with you?"

"Hi, Linc," Hadley spoke up from her seat. "Both Sophia and I are here. You should know Ryan wouldn't abandon us anywhere. I don't know him very well, but I have a feeling he's a very stubborn man."

"True. That's also what makes him a top-notch security specialist." Linc sighed. "Now, would one of you please tell me what's going on?"

Ryan quickly filled his business partner and best friend in on the events of the last hour. "So, you see, we had to move locations."

"Okay, but where are you going?"

The driver of the motor home in front of him put on their brakes as a family of elk crossed in front of them, and an idea came to Ryan. "Linc, we need to ditch my vehicle since our pursuer knows what it looks like, and I'm sure he's memorized my Colorado tag, too. Can you locate the closest RV rental place near me? Rent us a small motor home, and then find us a campground that allows off-season parking."

He could hear typing in the background as Linc searched the internet for an RV rental place.

"There's no need to do that," Hadley interjected. "I told you, Sophia and I could—"

"And I told you that wasn't going to happen." Frustration bubbled up inside him. She was a fine one to talk about how stubborn he could be. Didn't she know her stubbornness could go toe to toe with his any day? He shoved a hand through his hair. "Look, I know you're an independent person used to being on your own, but there's no need for you to face this alone."

"When you came to find me, you were only delivering the message that I no longer had to look over my shoulder for Troy. You didn't sign up for this."

"You're right, I didn't. But I'm not going to turn my back on the situation and leave you stranded, either."

"But it's Christmas. Don't you want to be with your family?"

"I want—"

"Okay, you two," Lincoln interrupted. "If you're finished arguing like an old married couple, I found you a place to hide."

Heat crept up Ryan's neck. He'd completely forgotten Linc was still on the phone, listening to their disagreement. Normally, he was a person of great control, and the fact that she could rattle him was a bit unnerving.

"Ryan? Hadley? Are y'all still there?"

Ryan cleared his throat and glanced at Hadley. Pink tinged her cheeks, indicating she, too, was embarrassed at their blunder. "Yeah. We're here. Sorry about that."

"No worries. Under normal circumstances, I'd find it entertaining. Ryan, it seems like you've found someone to match your stubborn streak." Linc laughed and then got serious. "Okay, so the closest campground that allows RV parking in the off-season is inside the Grand Tetons National Park. Which is a four-hour drive from your location."

"That's not good," Ryan sighed. "It will be dark soon."

"Exactly. However, I found an Airstream vacation rental that will work. It looks to be a four-acre campground with ten remodeled vintage Airstream campers that are set up as year-round vacation rentals. Unfortunately, you won't be able to ditch your vehicle. I wasn't able to find a rental available anywhere."

"It can't be helped. I'll be sure to park out of sight the best I can." Ryan rolled his shoulders, desperate to relieve some of the tension. "Book the Airstream."

"They only had one available, so I already booked it for three nights. I rented it under one of your aliases. I'll text the info to you along with the address. All you have to do is remember to give them the proper identification when you get there. You shouldn't have to pay anything since I prepaid with a Protective Instincts credit card."

Hadley gasped. "I'm sorry you had to do that. I promise to pay back every cent of what this is costing your company. Please send me the bill once this is over. And don't forget to bill me for Ryan's time, too."

Her words hit him like a sucker punch to the gut. Did she really think he wanted to be paid for his time?

"That's a negative. There won't be a charge for my time," Ryan said. "Oh, and Linc, I appreciate the offer of backup, but it would take you most of the night to get here. By then we should be settled in the campground. You and Bridge stay put. I'll call if I need you." He disconnected the phone before his friend could argue.

"Why did you tell him not to bill me for your time?"

"Would you bill a friend for helping them in a time of need?"

"No, but this is different. We're not friends, and I'm not a damsel in distress you need to ride in on your white horse and rescue."

"Any friend of Jessica's is a friend of mine. Since she's no longer around to help you, I'll take her place. No charge."

"Who is Jessica?" Sophia asked from the back seat.

He glanced in the rearview mirror and caught Sophia staring at him as she covered a yawn.

Hadley turned in her seat, reached across and patted Sophia's leg. "Jessica was a very nice lady who helped you and Mommy a long time ago. I'll tell you all about her when you're older."

I'll tell you about her when you're older. Ryan hoped that she did tell Sophia about the woman with the infectious laugh and big heart who sacrificed everything to save them. Jessica's legacy needed to live on. He could show Sophia the worn photograph he kept in his wallet. The photo had been taken at his parents' ranch in Blackberry Falls, Colorado—a quick weekend trip to spend time with family before his ninety-day deployment to the Middle East, his last tour of duty as a Marine Corps officer. It was an image of Jessica, frozen in time, perched on a fence rail, a daisy tucked behind one ear and a smile on her face.

Maybe when Sophia was older, he and Lincoln could tell her stories about Jessica and some of the antics they pulled. He caught his breath. When Sophia was older, would he even been part of her life? She was adorable, but did he really want to stay connected to Sophia and her mom after this? Hadley had made it perfectly clear that she was an independent woman who didn't need close friends. And while he'd love to see Sophia all grown up and the kind of woman she became, he needed to remember she was Troy's daughter, too. Ryan wasn't so sure he could handle staying connected with the constant reminder of all he'd lost at the hands of Sophia's biological father.

ELEVEN

An hour and a half later, Ryan backed his SUV behind an Airstream decked out in holiday lights, which would be home for the next few days. They would try to blend in as a family of three, but would stay mostly to themselves. Thankfully, their campsite was in one of the remote areas of the campground.

Before heading to the campground, Ryan had made a quick stop at a big-box retail store where they had purchased food and other supplies. At one point, Hadley had asked him to help Sophia choose a new coloring book and had disappeared down the next aisle. When she returned, Ryan noticed she had hidden a few toys in the bottom of the shopping cart.

If she'd seen the doll he'd concealed while she picked out Sophia a new pair of warm, footed pajamas she hadn't said anything. Ryan just hoped Hadley hadn't seen the small gift he'd picked up for her. He'd entertained Sophia with jokes and funny faces while Hadley paid for her purchases, and then Hadley had taken her daughter to the restroom located right across from the checkout, while he paid for the groceries and other supplies. Which had given him a chance to pay for his gifts without prying eyes. He'd even thought to add wrapping paper to his purchases at the last moment. The only response from Hadley when she'd returned from the restroom was a raised eyebrow before she deposited Sophia into the child's seat attached to the cart. He smiled at the thought of them opening his gifts in a few days. It had been a long time since he'd found so much joy in giving to others.

"Looks like our nearest neighbor is about forty yards away," Hadley said, pulling him from his thoughts.

He looked to where she pointed, barely making out another Airstream hidden behind a clump of trees. "Good. It won't be possible to avoid everyone, but at least we are in a somewhat private location where we can spend the majority of our time out of sight of prying eyes."

"Yay! Mr. Bamboo, we're camping! It's gonna be fun," Sophia squealed as Hadley released her from her car seat. "I've always wanted to go camping."

"Is that right?" Ryan laughed. "You've always wanted to go camping."

"Uh-huh. 'Cause I've seen Dora camp and it…" Sophia started talking fast, her words jumbling together, making it difficult to understand her.

He raised an eyebrow at Hadley. She whispered the word *cartoon* above Sophia's head, while the little girl talked about the rain forest or something. It was astounding how much the child reminded him of his sister Bridget.

His heart warmed at the thought of his fast-talking, can-do-anything, loyal and loving sister. They'd almost lost her a year ago when she'd been the target of a serial killer. Now she was a married woman. Who knew, maybe she'd bless him with a niece like Sophia one day in the near future.

"Okay, peanut," he said picking up the child to get her attention. "I'm glad you're excited but you will have to be a good listener and obey your mommy, and me, at all times."

"Peanut. I am not a peanut," Sophia said indignantly, obviously missing the point he was trying to make.

"I know that." He winked at her. "It's a nickname. Kind of like when your mommy calls you Sunshine when you wake up in the mornings."

Sophia's lips formed an O and then she squirmed to get down.

"Hang on," Hadley ordered, taking Sophia out

of his arms and holding her still. "Did you hear what Mr. Ryan said? You have to have your listening ears on while we are camping. Okay?"

"Okay, Mommy." Sophia nodded and kicked her feet to be set free.

Ryan kissed the top of her head, his lips brushing perilously close to Hadley's cheek pressed against her daughter's face. He pulled back and ruffled the child's hair. "There are only two rules. First, never get out of your mommy's sight or mine. And second, always do what we say without question."

"Okay, Uncle Ryan." The child laid her head on her mom's shoulder as she gave up the fight to be set down to run free.

The somber expression on Sophia's little face tore at his heart, but he knew without a doubt that if something happened to this sweet child, he'd never be able to get over the heartache it would cause.

Closing the small door that separated the only bedroom from the rest of the camper, Hadley glanced over her shoulder at her daughter napping on the bed, Mr. Bamboo hugged close. It was amazing how her child could see their home ransacked, go on the run with a stranger, move from a motel to a cabin to a camper and still sleep peacefully.

Obviously, she had done something right these past five years to give Sophia a sense of security even in the situation they currently found themselves in. Pride swelled inside her. *Pride goeth before destruction, and a haughty spirit before a fall.* The scripture from the preacher's sermon last week came to mind as if a gentle reminder to not be puffed up. *Message received, Lord. Thank You for blessing me with Sophia. I pray she always feels secure and has comfort in the knowledge that she will always be loved by me. And You.*

Hadley went to work and quickly wrapped the few gifts she'd picked up for her daughter, just in case they didn't make it home for Christmas. Then she reached into the bag and withdrew *the* last item. A leather wallet. She hoped Ryan liked the gift. Hadley wasn't even sure if he were a religious man. She'd never even seen him pray. If she'd had more time, maybe she could have picked out something a little more fitting of his tastes. Of course, she had no clue what things he liked. The wallet had caught her attention because it had Jeremiah 29:11 embossed on the cover. And she imagined, if Ryan had let the idea of capturing Troy haunt him for all these years, he might have forgotten the Lord knew the plans He had for Ryan's life.

She sighed and quickly wrapped the present,

tucking it behind Sophia's on the top shelf of the small closet. Then, after draping a fuzzy blanket over Sophia and kissing the top of her head, Hadley exited the bedroom.

Ryan was nowhere to be found inside the small camper, but there were remnants of pink wrapping paper with a glittery snowflake design scattered about the table. A smile tugged at her lips. She thought she'd seen him hide a toy for Sophia in the shopping cart. His kindness to her daughter was unexpected but very much appreciated.

Where had he gone? She looked out the windows but didn't see him anywhere. He wouldn't have gone far, would he? Unless someone had nabbed him. *Don't let your imagination run wild. He wouldn't have gone without a fight. You would have heard something.*

Best to stay busy and not let her fears take over. She found an empty shopping bag and started cleaning up the table.

The door to the camper opened, and Ryan clomped across the threshold. "Oh, I thought you were resting with Sophia."

Hadley shook her head, pressing her lips together to contain the joy that wanted to break free at seeing him. "Nope."

Ryan crossed to the table and picked up the scissors and tape. "Let me clear this mess."

"It's okay. I've got it. Where have you been? I didn't know you'd left." Hadley tried not to let the fear she'd felt at the thought that he'd left her and Sophia without a word unsettle her even more.

"Since Sophia has *always wanted to go camping*, I thought I'd gather a few small branches and twigs for the firepit. Let her get the full experience."

"But I looked out the windows and didn't see you." The desperation she heard in her own voice made her cringe.

He stilled. "Hey. You didn't think I'd deserted you, did you?"

"No." She ducked her head so he wouldn't see the tears in her eyes. Why was she being overly emotional? Her dad would tell her to *toughen up* and *develop a thick skin*. Hadley had spent the last six years trying to do just that.

Before she knew what was happening, Ryan moved to her side and lifted her face upward.

"Yes. You did." Using his thumb, he wiped at the tears that now ran freely down her cheeks. "I'm sorry. I never meant to scare you."

"It's okay." She hiccupped. "Deep down, I knew you wouldn't have gone far. I…let my imagination get the better of me…that's all."

Strong arms wrapped around her and pulled her close to a rock-solid chest. "It's only natural that you would. You expected a relaxing Christmas break with Sophia. Instead, you've been on a roller-coaster ride of danger, running from an unknown enemy."

He rubbed her back and whispered comforting words as if she were a child Sophia's age. She knew she should pull away, but it was nice having someone to lean on for a change. Except, having someone to lean on wasn't a luxury she could afford to get used to. Jumping back, she bumped her elbow on the counter.

"Ow." She rubbed the sore spot as she turned toward the back of the motor home. "I'll check on Sophia."

Ryan put out a hand on her arm. "About that, I'm sorry. It seemed like you needed a shoulder to lean on. I didn't mean anything…"

She scrubbed her hands across her face and finished drying her tears. "I know. Thank you."

Without another word, she turned and walked away. She would have to do a better job of hiding her emotions in the future. Having Ryan think she was a helpless, needy female wouldn't serve any purpose at all. His instinctive chivalrous desire to comfort a woman in distress would have him constantly wanting to comfort her. If she wanted to avoid—both herself and her daughter—getting too attached to the security specialist, she needed to put up boundaries until this ordeal was over. The sooner Ryan returned to Denver, the better. Which meant she needed to figure out who was after her. Fast.

TWELVE

Ryan watched Hadley disappear into the bedroom and close the door behind her. He knew he'd messed up.

Why was he letting his feelings get the better of him with this little family? Other than his mother and Bridget, he hadn't hugged another woman since Jessica's funeral. And then it had been an automatic response to others. He'd numbingly returned the embraces of the other mourners, knowing deep inside that none of them would want to comfort him if they knew he'd been the one to let her down. The reason Troy had been able to kill her in the first place. Jessica had begged him to elope prior to his last deployment. She said she didn't want them to be separated without being husband and wife, but he'd convinced her she deserved the grand wedding of her dreams and not to let fear make her do something she would later regret. He'd promised he'd come back to her and they'd live happily ever after.

If only he'd married her like she'd wanted, he could have moved her into base housing and Troy never would have been able to reach her that night.

Opening the small pantry cabinet, he found the box of matches he'd purchased when they picked up groceries and went outside to light the campfire. It was dark enough now that anyone driving past shouldn't be able to identify them, and he wanted Sophia to experience making s'mores. He'd have everything ready so they could have the treat after she awoke from her nap.

Ryan quickly set to work lighting the fire and then dropped down onto one of the rustic, Adirondack-style log chairs. "Dear Lord, I know I've not prayed as much as I should have these past few years. Actually, I've probably prayed more the past three days than I have since Jessica died. It's not that I blamed You. Honestly, I didn't want to talk to anyone, feeling like I had to be the one to make things right." He propped his elbows on his knees and put his head into his hand. "You know I've never been a person who believed in regret. Mistakes are the things that help us grow so we become better people. But why did I ignore Jessica's pleas? She was so afraid something would happen during my deployment, and we'd never make it to our wedding. Why did my deployment have to cost Jessica her life?"

A noise sounded behind him, and he spun to find Hadley, her hand on the doorknob, frozen like a statue, in the act of turning away from him. She gasped and covered her mouth with her hand. "I'm so sorry. I didn't mean to interrupt you…"

"It's okay. I was just—"

"Blaming yourself for Jessica's death."

He shrugged. "Yeah, well, if I had married her before my deployment like she wanted, she'd probably still be alive."

"You don't know that," she said matter-of-factly. "He could have cornered her at graduation the next day, and then other peoples' lives may have been put in danger, too."

Hadley closed the camper door, crossed over to the firepit and sat down on the chair closest to him. "If you need someone to blame for putting Jessica in the position to face Troy in the first place, then I'm the one you need to be mad at, not yourself."

"No. It's not your fault."

"It's more my fault than it is yours. I could have gone to the police, gotten a restraining order and faced Troy head-on… But instead, I ran and hid like a scared little child. And Jessica paid the price for my actions."

Lord, I didn't mean to make Hadley feel guilty. She had to protect her unborn child. Please help me make her realize that.

"Don't blame yourself. You weren't just protecting yourself. Sophia had to be a priority." He felt like such a heel for making her carry some of the weight of his own guilt.

A gloved hand covered his and squeezed. He jerked his head upward. Firelight danced across her face, illuminating her hazel eyes, and he could read the compassion inside them.

"I don't blame myself. I blame Troy. He's the one who couldn't control his emotions and lashed out, killing an innocent soul. Not me. And not you." She lifted one corner of her mouth in a half smile. "It's okay to feel remorse and to think about what could have been if we'd done things differently. But we can't go back and change things. Even if we could, we have no way of knowing if the outcome would be better or worse. So, instead of living in the past, it's better to live for the here and now. And hope and pray for a better future."

"How did you get so wise?"

"It comes with motherhood." She chuckled. "Seriously, I mess up every day. I've had to learn to give myself grace. And realize all bad things that happen aren't my fault, even when I feel remorse over them."

Her words settled over him like a warm, comforting blanket, assuaging his mind. There was no need for a reply, so they sat quietly watching the flickering flames of the fire. Muted sounds of people talking and playing at the campsites nearest them was like background music to the symphony of the crackling logs. Ryan was reminded of numerous family camping trips he'd taken with the Vincents after they'd adopted him. Before then, the closest he'd gotten to a camping trip was a night spent sleeping in a hammock on his neighbor's back porch. His mom, a single parent like Hadley, had done the best she could to provide for him. When she'd died, he'd felt so alone, until the Vincents came along and offered him a place in their family. God had blessed him with three loving parents. And because of the adoption, he'd gone from being an only child to a middle sibling with four brothers and a sister.

His thoughts drifted to the sleeping child in the camper. Would she ever get to experience the joys of having siblings? Not unless Ryan kept both her and her mother safe.

"Mommy!" Sophia cried, breaking the stillness.

"I was beginning to think she was down for the night." Hadley pushed to her feet, only taking a few steps before a scream pierced the air. "What in the world? She's never woken like that before." She took off running.

Ryan raced past her, bounding up the two metal steps leading into the camper, his heart pounding in his chest. It had been his experience that Sophia was always a happy child when she woke, a smile on her face. *Please, Lord, let the cause of the scream be a bad dream.*

Hadley was right on Ryan's heels as he darted through the door and down the length of the camper, past the living area, kitchen and tiny bathroom. Sophia's cries had stopped before they entered the trailer, but it didn't lesson his sense of urgency.

They reached the bedroom, and Ryan struggled to open the door. He could practically feel Hadley breathing down his neck as he sensed her urge to push him out of the way and rip the door off its track. But he knew that if he couldn't open the door, she wouldn't be able to, either.

"The door's caught on something," he said through clenched teeth.

"Let me help." She squeezed beside him and grasped the small plastic handle, pushing as he pulled. "Sophia, it's Mommy. Are you blocking the door?"

Silence.

"Sophia, answer Mommy!"

More silence. Ryan doubted Sophia was a child who ignored her mother. Unless she wasn't able to answer.

"We've got to get in there, even if it means tearing this door down," Hadley demanded.

"Agreed. I think we can bust through it if we hit it together, as hard as we can." He turned to her, and he saw fear in her hazel eyes that he was sure mirrored his own.

She nodded her agreement and he swallowed, unable to form words, his mind racing through the scenarios of what they'd find on the other side of the door.

They each took a step back and turned sideways, facing each other.

"Okay. Ready. Go!" Ryan ordered.

He rammed his right shoulder against the door, acutely aware of the burning sensation spreading down his arm. The door popped loose at the top on Ryan's side, but Hadley's side stayed completely intact. She grunted and hit it again, and again.

Ryan grasped her shoulders and pulled her back, guiding her to stand behind him. "We've weakened it enough I can kick it down now." *Please, Lord. Let this work.*

He braced his arms against the wall on either side of the narrow hall, lifted his legs and kicked both feet with force. The door popped open and fell against the bed.

He climbed over the door and pushed into the room.

"Sophia. Where are you?" Hadley demanded as she pressed past him.

Mr. Bamboo lay in the middle of the bed, the covers crumpled around him. A cool gust of wind blew across the room, sending a chill up Ryan's spine. The emergency escape window showed signs of having been pried open.

"Sophia!" Hadley cried and tried to brush past him.

"No. You can't go rushing out there, you'll get yourself killed. Stay—" He'd almost said *Stay here* but that wouldn't work. The shooter could circle back while he was out trying to find Sophia and get Hadley, too.

"You have to come with me. I can't leave you here unprotected."

"You better believe I'm coming with you."

"Listen." He grasped her upper arms and forced her to look at him. "The only way I can protect you and Sophia is if you follow my orders. Got it? If you rush out there recklessly, it could get you killed—"

"I don't care. I've got to—"

"Yes, you do. You don't want to leave Sophia without a mother. And if you do anything reckless, you could jeopardize her life, too." She visibly blanched, and he knew his words had had the desired effect.

He pulled out his phone and quickly typed out a text message, then put it on silent and slipped it back into his jacket pocket. "Okay, I just sent a text to nine-one-one, apprising them of the situation and our location. They'll notify the sheriff's department. We should have backup shortly." He reached behind his back for his gun, tucked into its holster in his waistband and headed for the door. "But we're not waiting around. They can't have gotten far. Let's go."

Ryan prayed he was right and Sophia would be back in her mother's arms within the hour.

THIRTEEN

They made their way out of the camper and crossed to the trail that wove through the woods to a stream. Hadley was thankful Ryan had insisted they explore the area adjacent to their campsite after they arrived. It seemed obvious this would be the way the kidnapper would've taken Sophia. If he had gone the other direction, he would've passed Hadley and Ryan. She silently berated herself. What had she been thinking, sitting outside by a campfire as if she were on vacation and not running for her life?

Her foot hit a rock, and she stumbled. Reaching out, she clutched the back of Ryan's jacket to stop her fall.

"Be careful." He half turned, grasped her elbow and righted her. "Do we need to slow our steps?"

"No. We can't. They're getting away." Fear and desperation made her words louder than she'd intended. "Please," she whispered. "Sophia will be scared. She's never been away from me at night."

"Okay, but hang on to me so you can keep your balance on this uneven ground." He turned back to the path, and she fisted his jacket in her hand, determined to keep up and not slow him down.

There was a smattering of stars in the sky, but the moon was completely hidden behind clouds that promised to dump another layer of snow by morning. Add in the thick woods they had just entered, and it was even more difficult to see. *Lord, please, we need You to guide our path. Don't let them hurt my baby.*

A child's cry sounded in the distance, and an icy chill snaked up her spine and seized her heart.

"Sophia!" She had to get to her daughter.

Hadley tried to push past Ryan, but he grasped her arm and pulled her close.

"Shhh. Listen," he whispered.

What was his problem? Didn't he understand her daughter needed her? She struggled, and he tightened his grip, his fingers biting into her flesh. She stilled.

The child screamed again, but it was instantly followed by laughter and an adult's voice saying, "Play quietly so you don't disturb the neighbors."

The screams had come from the children at the next campsite, who were playing hide-and-seek.

"How did you know it wasn't Sophia's scream?" she whispered.

Ryan let go of her arm and frowned. "The cry hadn't sounded like it was from a child who was hurt or scared."

He was right. How could she not differentiate a playful squeal from a scared cry? More than that, why hadn't she been able to tell it was a different child and not her own? A mother should know the sound of her own child's cries. The adrenaline that pushed her this far evaporated, and fear that she would never see Sophia again invaded her mind. Her body began to tremble, and she crossed her arms over her body and grasped her elbows, hugging herself tightly in a vain effort to control it.

Ryan pulled her against his hard chest, wrapping his arms around her and holding her firmly. "It's okay. You're frightened and you want your little girl back. Every sound is going to invoke a reaction. The important thing is to pause for one second and listen before reacting. We can't let them hear us coming."

Hadley nodded and pushed away from Ryan. "I'm okay now. Let's keep going."

They had only taken a few steps when the sound of a siren rent the air.

"Sounds like the police have arrived. We need to get back to the campsite and fill them in on what's happened." Ryan turned back the way they had come.

"What? No. They're getting away." What was he thinking? She had to keep going. If they lost the kidnapper's trail now, Hadley might never see Sophia again. This couldn't be happening. After all she'd been through to keep her child safe, how could she fail Sophia now?

"I understand that you think the best way to save Sophia is to follow them and hope to catch them. But the reality is that they have probably reached their vehicle by now. The only way we're going to stop them from leaving the area with her is if we can get the police to block all exits. Which means we have to go back to camp and talk to the authorities. Okay?"

His words were logical. Even though not tracking down the kidnapper like a momma lioness in the wilderness went against every instinct in her body, she knew he was right. The abduction of her daughter was bigger than anything she could handle. This time she couldn't save Sophia's life alone.

"I'm sorry I let my guard down and Sophia was taken. I promise I'll get her back, and I won't rest until the person who took her is in custody. Please, trust me," Ryan pleaded.

For the past three days he'd dedicated every waking moment to keeping them safe. She knew he wouldn't steer her wrong. He was right, she needed help from law enforcement, but what he didn't seem to understand was that the person she trusted to get them through this ordeal was him. The knowledge that at some point since the first attack Ryan had become her most trusted ally hit like a meteor.

"I do trust you. And I don't blame you for what happened." She headed back toward camp. "Now let's get all roads out of this area closed so we can get Sophia back."

They emerged into the clearing of the campsite as two deputies rounded the motor home, weapons drawn. "Hold it, right there," one of the officers commanded.

Hadley instantly froze and put her hands up, palms out. "We're the ones who called you. My dau—"

Ryan jostled against her. "Wait until we're inside," he whispered. "There's an audience."

She turned her head and saw people from other campsites emerging through the thicket of trees that were designed to offer privacy. Apparently, their curiosity had pulled them away from their warm campers and family games.

"May I?" Ryan pointed to his pocket. "My identification."

The male deputy nodded, and Ryan quickly handed over his identification. "Like my friend, Ms. Logan, said, we called you. This is our campsite. And this matter is urgent and requires quick action."

"The nine-one-one dispatch said there was a kidnapped child. The motor home door was open when we arrived and..." He nodded to the window at the back of the RV.

"Can we go inside and talk, where it's a little less public? Please?" Hadley asked.

Several of the campers huddled together, whispering. Their phones pointed in Ryan and Hadley's direction, obviously recording what was happening. If the person who took Sophia wasn't Parker or someone related to Troy, Hadley would prefer to keep her identity secret. No need advertising her whereabouts to Troy's family, or letting them know he had a child.

"Of course." The deputy turned to his female partner. "I'll go inside and take their statement. In the meanwhile, why don't you tell the gawkers over there to go back to their own campsites."

"On it," she replied and jogged toward the group of onlookers, several of whom scattered the moment they saw her headed in their direction.

Ryan, Hadley and the male deputy made their way into the Airstream. The minute she crossed the threshold and saw the bedroom door on the floor, Hadley's throat tightened and tears burned her eyes. This was taking too long, giving the kidnapper an even bigger escape window.

"Okay, someone tell me what happened." The deputy pulled a small notepad and pen from his shirt pocket.

Hadley nodded at Ryan, indicating that he should tell the events of the evening. She didn't trust herself to keep her emotions intact.

While Ryan filled the deputy in on the events that had transpired the past few days and the urgency of the situation, Hadley moved to the back of the Airstream. She picked up the door and propped it against the wall. Bits and pieces of the conversation between Ryan and the deputy drifted to her. The deputy appeared to be questioning if someone had taken Sophia or if she may have wandered off.

"She's five years old!" Ryan's voice rose, his frustration with the deputy evident. "You saw the emergency window. There's no way she was able to open it and climb out on her own without getting hurt. Even if she had, there's no way she would have gotten far in the dark. Her mother and I would have found her."

"Sir, I promise you, I want to find her, too. We never want any child to go missing, but I can't close every road in the surrounding area unless I have proof someone abducted her."

Hadley's eyes fell on her daughter's stuffed panda bear. Her knees buckled, and she sank onto the bed. "Oh, Mr. Bamboo," she whispered. "Why couldn't they have taken you, too? Sophia could use your comforting hugs."

A tear slid down her face, and she scrubbed it away with the palm of her hand. Picking up the beloved toy, she pulled him close, and a piece of paper fluttered to the floor. *What's this?* She bent and picked up the torn-out notebook page, flipped it over and gasped. Written with a black marker were the words: *Your daughter is safe, for now. I will notify you with my ransom demands.*

She rushed back to the dining area where Ryan and the deputy stood. "There's a ransom note. Contact the national guard, or FBI, or whomever you need to call, but get the roads leading out of this area closed. Now!"

His heart skipped a beat when Hadley held out a piece of torn notebook paper, not knowing if a ransom note was a good thing or a bad thing. It completely changed the dynamics of the situation—there was little doubt in his mind the abductor wasn't a member of Troy's family. This was going too far, even for them. However, even though they still had no clue who had taken

Sophia, the ransom note meant the kidnapper needed to keep Sophia alive as a bargaining chip.

Ryan read the note as the deputy peered over his shoulder. "They don't say what they want. No money amount or anything else. Why would they leave a note but no details?"

"I'm not sure, but this warrants blocking off all exits now." The deputy stepped outside to call for backup.

Hadley grasped the countertop, her face pale. "What am I going to do if they ask for a large ransom? I don't have that kind of money. Why are they doing this to me? My sweet Sophia, she must be so scared. They didn't even take her favorite toy…"

For the second time this evening, he pulled her into his arms, Sophia's giant panda squished between them as he held her tightly, desperately trying to offer her a sense of security. "We'll get her back. I'll call in my own cavalry. You and Sophia are officially clients of Protective Instincts. And we've never lost a client." *Yet. No, don't even go there.* Ryan forced all negative thoughts out of his mind. If his company were to fail on a protection assignment, it wouldn't be with the loss of a child. Especially a child who owned a piece of his heart.

The image of Sophia offering to share her fish-shaped crackers with him flitted across his mind.

Dear Lord, if we get her back—no, not if—when we get her safely home, I promise I'll eat any snack items she offers me. Anything to see that smile on her face and the light in her eyes.

Hadley stepped out of his arms, and he felt a cold void in her place. *Get it together, Vincent! You've developed too deep an attachment to this small family. Don't let it cloud your judgment. Do your job and then hightail it back to Denver.*

"I'm going to go find my phone. I need to keep it with me in case the kidnapper tries to contact me."

"Good idea. I'll call Lincoln and have him and Bridget head this way." Ryan pulled his cell phone out of his back pocket as he watched her disappear into the bedroom.

Linc answered on the second ring. The sound of traffic and road noise came across the line.

"Hi, Linc, I hope you're not headed anywhere important, because I need you here ASAP." Ryan shoved his hand through his hair. He hated to admit he'd messed up. "I shouldn't have told you not to come earlier. Things have taken a turn, and I really need the backup."

"Good thing we don't always listen to you, bro." Bridget laughed. "Linc, Sawyer and I are about two hours away. We would have been there already, but the snow has slowed us down."

Ryan's heart swelled at the love and sacrifice

of his friend and family, traveling so far to help him during the holidays.

"We were considering finding a couple of rooms for the night," Linc broke in. "But if we go slow and steady, we can probably make it to you in two or three hours."

"What's happened to make you change your mind about needing us?" Sawyer asked. Leave it to his levelheaded brother-in-law to get right to the point.

Ryan puffed out a breath. "Sophia has been abducted."

Bridget's gasp came across the line. "Oh no. Poor Hadley."

"Yeah, she's doing a pretty good job of holding it together, but we need to find Sophia fast. The kidnapper left a note saying they'd be in touch with their ransom demands."

"How long has she been gone?" Linc asked.

"I'd say about forty-five minutes."

"Did you report it?" Sawyer inquired.

"Yes, but it took a while to convince the deputy she was taken and hadn't just wandered off. They're trying to get the roads out of the park closed off now…" Ryan's voice broke. "I just pray it's not too late. The kidnapper could be long gone by now."

"You and Hadley stay strong. We'll be there as quickly as we can," Sawyer said in his calm,

FBI agent voice. "In the meantime, I'm calling the Bureau to ask for their immediate assistance. Given Sophia's age, they should respond quickly."

"Thanks, Sawyer." Even as he said the words, Ryan heard Sawyer talking to someone else in hushed tones in the background.

"He's on the phone with an FBI friend," Bridget said softly. "Hang in there, Ryan. We'll be there as quickly as we can. And in the meantime, we'll be praying."

"Thanks, Bridge." Both deputies stepped back into the motor home as Ryan disconnected his call.

"I've contacted the local police departments. They're going to barricade the roads and search all vehicles trying to exit the area," the male deputy who'd been so difficult earlier informed him.

"No!" Hadley rushed out of the bedroom, her cell phone in her hand.

"What is it?" Ryan took the phone to see what had frightened her. It was a text message from an unknown sender.

I want $150,000. To be dropped off at a location near Foster Falls at noon tomorrow. I'll contact you with the exact location later.

"Tomorrow is Christmas Eve, and it's a Sunday. How can the kidnapper expect us to pull that together?"

Hadley sank onto the dinette bench, propped her elbows on the table and put her head in her hands. "Even if I didn't have those two things working against me, there's no way I could come up with that kind of money. I'm a school teacher, not a millionaire."

"We'll figure something out. Hopefully, we'll catch the guy before you ever have to turn over any of the money." Ryan turned to the deputies. "Foster Falls is a three-hour drive. If the person who took Sophia is headed there with her, maybe he can be intercepted on one of the routes."

"I'll radio the information in," the male deputy responded. "However, I must caution you not to get your hopes too high. We can't stop every vehicle between here and Foster Falls. If our perp changed vehicles…"

A repetitive, piercing beep erupted from Hadley's cell phone, quickly followed by the other three cell phones in the room. "That's probably the Amber Alert," the female deputy said.

Ryan looked at his phone screen and saw the details of the alert.

WHITE FEMALE. AGE FIVE. UNKNOWN ABDUCTOR. SUSPECT COULD BE TRAVELING IN A SILVER KING CAB CHEVROLET TRUCK.

"I may never see my baby again," Hadley cried, dropping her phone on the table.

Ryan turned and asked the deputies to step outside and give them a minute. Then he sat down opposite Hadley and picked up her hand. "Don't let your mind go there. Linc, my sister Bridget and her husband were already on their way here when I called them. They'll be here in a few hours. And Sawyer—my brother-in-law—is an FBI profiler. He'll be able to help us figure out who is behind this. And he's already called the Bureau to request their help on this. We will get her back."

"What if—"

"Don't fall down the what-if hole. It's a dark, scary place that you don't need to be right now." He squeezed her hand. "If you'd let what-ifs control your thinking six years ago, you never would have escaped Troy."

"Yes, but then Jess—"

"No. No buts. Pull from your struggles and life lessons. They can either make you a stronger person or shatter your confidence into a million tiny pieces." He lowered his voice so his words would have more impact. "Over the course of the last few days, I've witnessed your strength. You've faced every obstacle with faith and determination. Don't give up now."

She looked up, tears shimmering in her eyes.

"Can we pray, together? I can't do this without you and God."

Though he had never intentionally turned his back on God, Ryan had distanced himself from Him and his church family. Once, he'd been an active member of the congregation, leading the song service and offering prayers on behalf of the assembly. *Lord, give me the right words to say to comfort Hadley.*

Ryan looked at Hadley's expectant expression, swallowed the lump in his throat, nodded and bowed his head. "Our kind and most holy heavenly Father. We pray that you will give us the strength to endure the road we are traveling. Please, protect Sophia and comfort Hadley as only You can…"

FOURTEEN

"Amen," Hadley echoed Ryan as she hugged Sophia's stuffed animal close, her anxiety easing for the first time since they'd discovered Sophia missing. "Thank you for leading the prayer. In situations like this it's easy to forget Who is in control."

He offered her a half smile, his face showing remorse. "Actually, I needed the reminder, too. Now, let's make a plan to—"

"What's this?" She pressed the stuffed panda's right ear between her fingers. "There's something hard inside Mr. Bamboo's ear."

"Let me see." Ryan took the beloved toy and placed it on the table.

In the light, Hadley could see a loose gray thread that didn't match the rest of the threads. Grasping the end, she pulled it loose, and a small white square piece of plastic dropped onto the table.

"Tracking device. No wonder they found us everywhere we hid," Ryan stated flatly.

"How were they able to put it in there without my knowledge?"

"I'm not sure, but I do know one thing. This is proof that the person responsible is someone you know and have been in contact with in the last week or so."

Her phone rang. Carlton McIntyre's name flashed on the screen, and she gasped. "I forgot about Carlton. He's the only person I know who might be able to get the money for the kidnappers."

She reached for the phone, but Ryan grabbed it before she could. "Why would he be calling at this time of night? How can you be sure he's not involved in this?"

"Don't be silly. Why would he want to harm Sophia? We've been going out to his ranch for riding lessons for months. If he'd wanted to snatch her, he had better opportunities than this. Besides, he is the last person to need money like that. And he knows I don't have that kind of cash." The phone rang for the third time. She held out her hand, expectantly.

"Okay, but we put it on speaker." Ryan slid his finger across the screen to answer the call, and then pressed the speaker symbol.

Hadley took a deep breath and released it, in hopes her voice would sound normal. "Hello?"

"Hadley, is everything okay? You ended our phone conversation abruptly earlier, and I just saw an Amber Alert for a five-year-old girl. I'm worried about you and Sophia. Tell me you're both fine," he demanded.

"Now, Daddy, settle down. The odds of it being Sophia are very slim," Carlton's daughter, Mikael McIntyre, said in the background. "Give Hadley a chance to answer. You'll see."

How much should she share? She looked to Ryan for guidance. He nodded. Hadley swallowed. "Actually, the Amber Alert child is Sophia."

"What!" Carlton roared, and Hadley could picture his calloused hands fisted at his side and a pensive expression on his weathered face. "Who took her? What can we do to help you get her back? Have you called the FBI?"

"Shhh... Daddy, let her speak," Mikael scolded. "Go ahead, Hadley, fill us in on the details."

"There aren't many details to share," Ryan spoke up.

"Who's that? Is it the police? Why are you sitting around doing nothing? Get out there and find my little sweetheart."

"Daddy. You're not helping."

"Mikael's right, Carlton. You don't need to get so worked up." Hadley looked at Ryan and shook her head. She had grown very fond of Carlton McIntyre over the past few months as he'd stepped into the role of grandparent to both her and Sophia. He could be gruff and a bit high-handed, but he had a big heart.

"The man with me is my friend Ryan from Colorado. He's been helping me and Sophia out the past few days. We have everything…" She started to say *under control* but that wasn't true, was it? "We're doing everything we can to get Sophia back quickly. Try not to worry."

"Don't concern yourself with Daddy," Mikael interjected. "I'll take care of him. But if you need anything—a place to stay while you search for Sophia or anything else—we're here for you."

"Actually," Ryan said. "You might be able to help us with something."

"Name it. Anything at all," Carlton asserted.

"The kidnapper has demanded a ransom to be paid tomorrow."

"What!"

"How much?" Mikael and Carlton said in unison.

"One hundred fifty thousand." Hadley held her breath.

"I'll have it for you by morning," Carlton said.

"You can't do that," Mikael insisted.

"You shush now. I can do anything I want with my money. Sophia and Hadley are fam... like...family."

"But Daddy—"

"Hadley," Carlton said, cutting off his daughter, "you and that friend of yours come to the ranch bright and early in the morning. I'll have the funds for you."

The line went dead, and Hadley slumped back against the dinette bench cushion, dazed. "I honestly didn't think it would be that easy to get so much money. I knew he had to be well off—I've seen his ranch, house and vehicles—but getting that kind of money...like that..." She snapped her fingers.

"Agreed. The few people I know who could possibly get their hands on that kind of cash would definitely need more than fifteen hours' notice." He took his glasses off and rubbed his eyes as she'd seen him do numerous times when he was in deep thought. "How can we be sure McIntyre and his daughter aren't involved in this?"

An involuntary gasp escaped her lips. "Why would you say that? Carlton loves Sophia. He'd never do anything to harm her. And Mikael is a bit standoffish, but I don't think she's being rude or anything. She's at least ten to fifteen years older than I am, and we don't have much in common. I'm a high school teacher. She's a rancher. I'm a young mother. She's never had a child. Actually, I think that may be why Carlton took up with Sophia and I. He knows his chances of having grandchildren of his own drops with each passing year. Besides, why offer up the money to pay your own ransom? What would that accomplish?"

"You're right. I'm simply at a loss as to who this person is." He put his glasses back on and peered at her. "Quite honestly, I thought you were his target. The attack at your home. The drive-by shooting. Following you at the outlet mall."

"I agree the drive-by shooting is a bit confusing if the goal the entire time was to kidnap Sophia for a ransom. They could have easily hit her, and…" A cold shiver snaked up her spine and choked the rest of her words, preventing them from being said aloud.

Ryan, always ready to offer comfort when needed, covered her hand with his and gave a gentle squeeze. What would she have done if he weren't here helping her navigate this nightmare?

Her phone dinged, indicating she'd received a text message, and fear immobilized her. "I can't look. What if it's the kidnapper?"

With one last squeeze of her hand, Ryan picked up the phone, turned it toward her so the face recognition software would unlock the screen, and then opened the message. "It's from Carlton."

He placed the phone on the table so they could read the text together.

Sorry I got off the phone without saying good-bye. If you need a place to stay tonight, you and your friend are welcome here. Call me if you need me, no matter the time. I love you and my sweet Sophia. Carlton.

She picked up her phone and typed a reply.

Thank you for your generosity. Sophia and I love you, too.

"Meeting Carlton and getting to know him and his daughter—well, all the staff at the ranch really—has been such a blessing. I was afraid Sophia was too young for riding lesson, but she has thrived." The memories made Hadley smile, her first real smile since this ordeal began.

"I imagine most kids would love to take riding lessons."

"I have to admit, I've been a bit of a helicopter mom since Sophia was born. Always afraid Troy would find us and take her. It was difficult to let her out of my sight. Even when selecting a daycare to enroll her in, I looked for one that offered access to live cameras so I could check on her throughout the day." She frowned. "Although I tried to hide my fears and not frighten Sophia, I'm afraid my actions made her become a very shy little girl who was terrified of shadows at every corner. But going to the ranch and having the freedom to roam around the stables with the ranch hands gave her a bit of independence I didn't even realize she needed."

"So you let her hang out in the stables without you?"

"Well, yeah, but not until I became familiar with the place myself, and never alone. She always had Mikael with her. And Mikael is great with kids. She has given riding lessons to all the kids in Eagle Creek through the years."

"But what do you know about the other ranch hands? Could one of them be behind the abduction?" Ryan pressed her for answers.

"I… I don't know…" She looked at Ryan, realization dawning that she had failed as a parent. How could she not know all the people her daughter had come in contact with on the ranch? "We need a list of Carlton's employees. Do you think your brother-in-law's contacts could run background checks for us?" Hadley gasped. "We need to get to the ranch. What if the abductor is an employee and they took Sophia back to the ranch? It's a huge spread with lots of places to hide a little girl."

The camper door opened and the female deputy poked her head inside. "Folks, there's a couple of FBI agents here to speak with you. Since this is a child abduction, they're going to take the lead on the investigation."

"We've been expecting them. Thank you," Ryan said. "Please tell them they can come in."

He turned back to Hadley. "I need you to stay strong. It could take us a few days to find Sophia, but I promise we won't give up, no matter how long it takes. I will see you and your daughter reunited." Ryan covered her hand once more. "Remember, I'm the guy who will go to the ends of the earth to seek justice for the people I love."

The people I love. He loved them? No. Well, Sophia, probably. She was a very lovable little girl who, since emerging from her shell in recent months, had wrapped many people around her cute little finger, including the man sitting across from Hadley.

Hadley could only pray Ryan was right and they would indeed find her daughter. And hopefully, the person who abducted her and spent the past three days tormenting them would be put in jail. Then they could go back to living normal lives. Well, optimistically, better than their old normal, since Troy was now out of the picture for good.

* * *

People I love. Now, why had he gone and said that? He didn't love Hadley. Sure, she was beautiful, and the first woman he'd hugged since Jessica's death, and even on the run from an unknown assailant, she'd been an easygoing person to be around. And Sophia was so much like Bridget it would be impossible not to adore her. But love? No. That had been a slip of the tongue. Surely, Hadley knew that. Right?

Two men dressed in street clothes entered the motor home and introduced themselves as Agent Parsons and Agent Fowler.

Ryan stood and held out his hand. "I'm Ryan Vincent, and this is the missing child's mother, Hadley Logan."

Both agents shook Ryan's hand and then Agent Fowler turned to Hadley. "Ma'am. I'm sorry we're meeting under these circumstances."

"Is there any news at all? Were the local police able to block off the exits?" Hadley pressed the agents for answers.

"They set up roadblocks. But I'm afraid they were probably too late in executing the plan. They've searched every vehicle leaving the area and there have been no children fitting your daughter's description. They've also not seen a vehicle that fits the description of the one that

Agent Eldridge said was seen at your home and trailing you the last few days."

"Agent Eldridge, Sawyer, is my brother-in-law," Ryan clarified for Hadley. "Do you know Sawyer, Agent?"

Agent Fowler nodded. "We went through the academy together. He's one of the best." Turning back to Hadley, he asked, "Do you have a photo of Sophia? It would be helpful to distribute it to law enforcement in surrounding areas and news outlets."

"I do, but…" Hadley turned tortured eyes on him and he could almost see her internal struggle. She had to do whatever it took to save Sophia, but she'd spent the past five years guarding Sophia's true identity. Would her photo, even with a different name, alert Troy to the existence of his daughter?

"Is there something else we should be aware of?" Agent Parsons queried.

"No." Ryan held up a finger. "Give us just one second."

He guided Hadley to the bedroom.

"I know this is hard," he said in hushed tones, "but you can't believe Troy will know the minute he sees Sophia that she is his child?"

"Why not? You did," she replied. "Don't try and deny it. I saw it in your face. You looked like someone had sucker punched you."

"Yes, but I knew your connection to him, so it was only logical that I'd pick up on the facial features. To Troy or anyone else, she's just another child. And since he doesn't even know about her existence, it's not like he's going to recognize her name. Which I should also point out is a different surname than the one he knew you by." He put two fingers under her chin and lifted her face so she could see into his eyes, and hopefully read the trust he had in the process that they'd have to follow to get Sophia back.

"I know you're right. I've had to be guarded for so long that it's difficult to let go of control."

"I get it. But you're not alone any longer. You have me. I won't just disappear once this is over. If Troy, or his family, figures out Sophia's connection to him and tries to take Sophia from you, Protective Instincts and all of our connections will do everything in our power to stop him, or them. You are Sophia's mom. Her only family. I won't let anyone else come in and lay claim to her."

"Thank you. I don't deserve your kindness." She swallowed. "Okay, let's get Sophia's image blasted across every news channel in the nation. I want my little girl back in my arms."

Hadley pulled out her cell phone and went back into the main area of the camper. "Here are the photos I have on my phone. Can I text or email them to you?"

Ryan followed behind her, silently praying he was right and hadn't just opened up a new box of trouble for Hadley and Sophia.

Forty-five minutes later, after the deputies and agents all left, Ryan and Hadley were alone in the quiet camper. He stood, propped against the small kitchen counter, and watched Hadley. She sat in the recliner with Mr. Bamboo clutched in her arms, a defeated expression on her face that tugged at his heart. He knew the powerless feeling of not being able to help the one you loved most in the world, the downward spiral of loss.

Although she had every right to wallow in grief and despair, Ryan knew from experience it was the worst thing she could do. How many months had he wasted in a dark hole he couldn't dig himself out of after Jessica's death? Six or seven? He couldn't remember. All he knew was those months had given Troy the perfect opportunity to go underground, making it even harder to locate him.

It had been two hours since Sophia was taken. They couldn't afford to sit here and grieve. There would be time for that if…no, he would not let his mind go there. They would find Sophia. No matter what it took. Ryan would see to it that she was back in her mother's arms by Christmas. Two days.

He crossed over to Hadley and held out his hand. She looked at him and frowned. "What?"

"We need to figure out who took Sophia."

"How are we supposed to do that? We've spent the last three days trying to figure out who was chasing us. We failed. And because of our failure, my daughter is now missing." She jumped to her feet and pushed him in the chest, tears streaming down her face. "You know what? I was wrong. This is your fault. If it wasn't for you, I would have hopped on a plane to Timbuktu or some other far-off place."

She drew back to hit his chest again, but he caught both of her wrists and pulled her into his arms, holding tightly as she cried. "It's okay. Let it all out," he whispered, rubbing her back. "You have every right to be angry. I let you down, but it won't happen again. We will figure this out."

He continued to whisper soothing words to her, and soon, her sobs turned to sniffles. Afraid to upset her again, he proceeded to hold her and offer comfort.

A quiet stillness settled over them, and after several long minutes, Hadley pulled back, a look of pure shame on her face. "I'm sorry. There's no excuse for my behavior. I know none of this is your fault. If I'd stayed with her instead of—"

"Hold it right there." He bent slightly at the waist so they'd be face-to-face. "No self-blame allowed, for either one of us. If we get caught in the if-only trap, we'll both be so busy digging ourselves out from under our individual guilt that we could miss the opportunity to catch the person responsible, and we won't be able to get Sophia back quickly."

She visibly blanched at his words, and he instantly regretted his bluntness. He wanted to motivate her into action, not scare her with the thought of never seeing Sophia again.

Lord, help me. I'm struggling to find the right words to comfort this hurting momma. Please, bless both of us with the peace of mind needed so we can look at the evidence clearly and catch the person responsible.

Ryan needed to reunite mother and daughter quickly. Failure was not an option. Otherwise, he was sure he'd fall into a pit of self-doubt so deep he might never get out again.

FIFTEEN

"That's it. Those are the names of the people who work on the ranch that Sophia and I have had interaction with." Hadley held out the notepad to Ryan.

He accepted the list and looked over it, hoping something would jump out at him—though he wasn't sure what, since he wouldn't know any of the names. "Not that I think it matters much, but what is each person's job on the ranch and how much interaction did you both have with each?" He knew he was grasping at straws here, but maybe something would jog her memory.

To his surprise, she didn't argue or say it was a waste of time. Instead, she picked up the pen and started filling in the details. "Joyce is the cook. Alexandria Emerson is the housekeeper. Gus is the ranch foreman. Desmond and Timothy are stable hands." She used the pen to point to names on the notepad as she continued. "We saw Joyce every time we visited. She insisted on feeding us, no matter what time of day it was. Said we were too skinny." Hadley smiled and then bit her lip.

He patted her hand. "Hey, it's okay to have happy memories, even in the darkest of times. It's those moments of light that give us hope."

She nodded. "I know you're right. It's just…it's so hard. I miss my baby. I know she's scared. But I wonder if she's warm. Has she been fed? Are they trying to entertain her so she isn't frightened?" She looked up at him, a broken woman whose light had been extinguished. "Are you sure it wasn't Troy's brother who took her? Dear Lord, I almost pray it was, because then at least she was taken by family. And surely any blood kin would love her and provide for her the way I would."

Words of comfort froze on his lips. He knew he needed to reassure her, but he couldn't. Not when he knew all families weren't light and love. Some were dark and filled with jealousy. His own father had run out on him and his mother when he was just a child of six. The last words he'd heard his dad say were, *I'm sick and tired of that brat coming before me. I told you I never wanted kids, but you had to go and have one anyway. Well, I hope you're happy, because you can raise him without me. I'm out of here.* His father had slammed out of the door and his mother had chased after him, tears streaming down her face as she begged him to return. He hadn't. And something had changed in Ryan's mother that night. She still treated him with great care and told him daily that she loved him, but somehow, he knew her love had changed and wasn't as deep as it had been before his dad left. His father had taken a big piece of her heart with him.

Even so, he knew without a doubt that no love ran as deep as a mother's love. Maybe it was because she carried the child under her heart for nine months. Or because she carried them in her arms during their infancy and toddler years. But at this instant, he knew he loved Sophia, too. He could not imagine life without her. Even after this entire ordeal was over and he had reunited mother and child and they were safe once again, he knew he'd want to keep in touch and be there for important occasions, her first father-daughter dance at school—if she'd let him be a stand-in— and then her high school graduation and wedding.

If he didn't get her back, he could never experience any of those things with her. Of course, if Hadley ever married, her husband might have something to say about Ryan's involvement. He pushed that thought far from his mind, refusing to analyze what part of that scenario bothered him more, the thought of Hadley marrying someone or the thought of someone else taking care of Sophia as his own. He swallowed the lump in his throat. "Try not to let your mind go there. All we can do is pray she's safe and warm, and work as hard as we can to get her back. Now tell me about the men you've put on the list."

"We only saw Gus and Timothy in passing. They were usually busy with chores, but Desmond was always hanging around the stables and corral while Sophia had her riding lessons from Mikael."

"Desmond didn't have other things he needed to be doing besides watching a five-year-old learning to ride?"

"He had an office in the stables, where he did paperwork, ordered supplies and planned out the job list for the day. He told me watching Sophia learn to ride was a pleasant break in his workday. Said her laughter and joy while riding was contagious and too much of a distraction to allow for much work. That's why he usually made sure the other workers were busy somewhere else on the property when we'd visit… He didn't want them being distracted and not getting their work done."

Ryan could picture Sophia sitting atop a Thoroughbred, her hair flying behind her as she rode, commanding the horse to do her bidding in the corral. "I can understand that. I'm sure the sight of her on a horse is a sight to see. She's such a tiny little girl… Did I tell you, when I first saw her sleeping in her car seat, I thought she was three and a half, maybe four, but definitely not five years old?"

Hadley smiled. "I hear that all the time. She is petite. I never met Troy's parents, but I saw photos. His mother is a petite woman, too. I'm sure that's where Sophia gets her size from." Her shoulders slumped. "Do you think it's wrong of me to keep Sophia away from her only grandparents? When I ran from Troy, I didn't even think about the other people I was robbing from being a part of my child's life."

"I think you did what you needed to do in order to keep both you and Sophia safe." He absentmindedly laced his fingers through hers. "After this is all over, if you want to reach out to Troy's parents and let them be part of Sophia's life, I'd be happy to go with you and talk to them."

As soon as the words were out, he wished he could yank them back. Not that he didn't want to support Hadley and be a shoulder for her to lean on. But he didn't need to be inserting himself into her life like he belonged there. How had the simple task of delivering good news to a woman in hiding turned into something so tangled and dangerous—not only to his life, but also to his heart?

* * *

A little while later Ryan received a text from his sister, letting him know they were about to pull into the campground. He went out to greet them, but Hadley stayed behind, knowing Ryan had things to discuss with his business partners and needing a few minutes to herself to process the mess her life had become the past few days. She needed to compose herself before she met Bridget, Sawyer and Lincoln. How would the latter feel about her? It was her fault his sister had been murdered. Would he resent her for Jessica's death? Guilt assaulted her and self-doubt creeped into her subconscious. Why were these people helping her? She was undeserving of their protection.

A faint knock sounded on the door Ryan had exited a few moments earlier, and a woman with beautiful auburn hair poked her head inside, made eye contact with her and smiled.

"Hi, ya," she said, stepping into the camper and pulling the door closed behind her. "I'm Bridget or Bridge, or if Ryan is in a particularly joking mood, Peanunchkin." She rolled her eyes, but the smile never left her face.

"Peanu—"

Bridget held up her hand, stopping Hadley. "I'll explain that particular nickname when we have a little more time." She crossed over and sat down in the small dining booth opposite her. "We have more important things to take care of first." Bridget's eyes searched hers, and Hadley had to resist the urge to squirm, sitting silently while waiting on the other woman to speak. "This is good. You're a tough lady, aren't you? There is sadness," she said, talking rapidly, not expecting a reply to her question, "but there is also a fire in your eyes—anger at your daughter's kidnappers or anger at yourself... I'm not sure—but I can already tell one thing about you. You're not letting your emotions control you."

Hadley scoffed. "You didn't see the puddle my tears made earlier."

"You cried them, and you released them. That's good. I like you. And I have no doubt, with your strength and determination, we'll figure out who took Sophia and get her back." Bridget leaned back and smiled.

Ryan's sister silently continued her assessment of her, until Hadley couldn't withstand the scrutiny any longer. "I don't know whether to thank you or be insulted that you're coming in here scrutinizing me."

"I'm sorry if it appeared like I was scrutinizing you. That was not my intention." She sighed and the corners of her mouth turned down. "Ryan and Sawyer are always telling me I'm too blunt. I don't mean to be. I've just always

been a person who calls things like I see them."
Bridget shrugged. "Oh, and I talk too fast."

That one statement drove home the realization
that Hadley was looking at a grown-up version
of Sophia. Blunt and to the point, speaking what
was on her mind, with a heart of gold that would
never purposefully hurt anyone.

Laughter bubbled up inside her, starting softly
and increasing in volume until she was doubled
over gasping for air. Every time Hadley thought
she had finally gathered her composure, she'd
look up at the shocked expression on Bridget's
face and erupt into a fit of laughter and tears.
She knew she was nearing hysteria but couldn't
seem to regain her composure. It was like someone had opened the floodgates of a dam and all
of her emotions were rolling out in a gush.

The door of the trailer opened and three men
pushed into the room, concern etched on their
faces. Ryan knelt beside Hadley and threw an
accusatory look at Bridget. "What did you say
to her?"

"Nothing. I was praising her for being a strong
woman and telling her we'd get Sophia back. Then
this happened." She gestured toward Hadley.

"Hadley, sweetheart, look at me. Focus."
Ryan put his hands on either side of her face
and turned her head toward him.

As she looked into his deep blue eyes, a blanket of calmness settled over her. She forcibly swallowed, and her laughter turned to a fit of hiccups.

"Someone, get her a glass of water," Ryan commanded the room at large, never taking his eyes off her.

Tears streamed down her face as if she were a leaky faucet. She tried to scrub them away with the back of her hand, but Ryan pulled a handkerchief out of his pocket, pushed her hand away and dried her cheeks. "I didn't think men carried handkerchiefs anymore," she said between hiccups.

"Most don't, but Grandpa Vincent taught me to be a true gentleman years ago." He smiled and accepted the water one of the men held out to him. Offering the glass to her, he added, "Maybe I'll tell you that story one day, but not now. We have more important things to take care of at the moment."

Hadley nodded and heat crept up her neck. "I'm sorry. I don't know what happened."

She turned to survey the people huddled around her. Bridget still sat across from her, a look of concern mixed with amusement on her face. A tall brown-haired man stood behind her, his hands on Bridget's shoulder. That must be her husband, Sawyer, the former FBI profiler. Standing between Sawyer and Ryan was a man Hadley would have recognized anywhere. Lincoln Jameson. She'd seen his picture on the wall in Jessica's apartment, just like she had Ryan's. But even without that, she felt like she would have known him by the similarities in his and his sister's facial features. Realizing she was staring, she quickly turned away. "I'm sorry."

"It's okay. I know I resemble my sister. Well, technically, since I am older, she resembled me."

"I for one don't see the resemblance. Jessica was way cuter." Ryan pushed to his feet, held out his hand to Hadley and helped her up. Then he turned toward the group. "Everyone, this is Hadley Logan, formerly known as Emma Bryant. Hadley, this is Lincoln and Sawyer. You've met my sister, Bridget, whom I want a word with in private."

Hadley put her free hand on his arm. "Please, there's no need for you to be upset with Bridget. She didn't do anything wrong. She actually complimented me on my strength during a difficult situation."

"Then, what happened?" Bridget stood, forcing Lincoln to take a step backward.

Thankful that Ryan still held tightly to her hand because she didn't want to lose the strength the small contact gave her, she smiled at his sister. "There wasn't anything wrong with what you said. Actually, I was amazed at your candor. I imagine most people would want to tiptoe around the situation and offer what they thought was soothing reassurance. When you finished and you sat back looking at me, waiting on my response, it hit me that I was getting a glimpse into my future."

"How so?" the petite redhead asked.

"You are a grown-up version of my sweet—"

"Sophia."

She and Ryan spoke in unison.

Hadley turned to Ryan and he smiled. "From the first moment I met Sophia, I have been struck by her similarities to Bridget. Maybe that's why she quickly stole a piece of my heart."

A lump formed in her throat and her heart swelled. Ryan loved her child. This was a good thing, right? If he had a strong connection to the missing person, wouldn't he work twice as hard to find her and bring her back? Yes, but it also meant it was very likely Sophia had developed strong feelings for Ryan, too. Hadley had failed at protecting her daughter's emotions. Realization dawned and she pulled her hand from his grasp. She'd failed to protect her own emotions, too. There would be a mess of feelings to pack away once the handsome bodyguard walked out of their lives, but she couldn't worry about that at the moment. First things first. Her daughter was in danger and they had to find her fast.

SIXTEEN

It was after midnight, and Ryan sat outside alone by the campfire pit, poking the logs and doing his best to ignite the embers that remained from the fire he and Hadley had sat around earlier.

Bridget had convinced Hadley to lie down and rest, telling her that even if she couldn't fall asleep, simply lying quietly and allowing her body to recharge would give her the strength to get through the ordeal she would face tomorrow. He prayed Hadley had quieted her mind long enough to fall asleep. Ryan's soul ached at the thought of Sophia, alone and scared, in the hands of the people who'd stolen her.

He'd only loved Sophia a few days, and he was tormented by his failure to protect her. He couldn't imagine the anguish Hadley was going through. She had protected Hadley from a father that hadn't wanted her to even take her first breath; she had loved her and nurtured her alone as a single parent all these years. Earlier, he'd told Hadley they couldn't let their minds wander down the what-ifs trail, but sitting alone in the cold, dark night, he could no longer ignore the possibility they might not get Sophia back. If that happened, how would Hadley survive the grief? For that matter how would he?

Picking up two split logs he dropped them a little too forcefully onto the fire. Sparks flew into the air.

"Are you sure it's a good idea to build a big fire at this time of night?" Bridget said, coming up behind him.

He'd let her sneak up on him. *Get your head in the game, Vincent. Just because your backup arrived doesn't mean you don't have to be alert at all times.*

"Probably not, but I don't imagine I'll get much sleep tonight anyway. Did Hadley fall asleep?"

"Yes, thankfully." Bridge settled into the same seat Hadley had sat in earlier and shame washed over him. If only he had stayed alert. Or better yet, if he'd stayed locked inside the motor home with both Sophia and Hadley, as he should have, the little girl would be inside, sound asleep in her mother's arms.

"Stop."

Ryan looked at his sister. "Stop what?"

"By the look on your face, I'd say you've been

berating yourself for Sophia's disappearance. You've only recently learned to bury the regret you felt over losing Jessica, even though that, just like this, wasn't your fault."

"But you're wrong. This time it is very much my fault. I should have been able to stop it from happening." He kicked at a small rock. "I let my guard down. Instead of being on guard inside the camper, I was out here, building a campfire for s'mores." The admission stung. He'd always been proud to be someone for his sister to look up to, but now she'd know the reason he worked in the background at Protective Instincts was because he couldn't hack it as a bodyguard.

Bridget leaned forward and propped her elbows on her knees. "I have a few questions, and I want you to answer them quickly, without taking time to ponder the right or wrong answer. Okay?"

He chuckled. "You sound like your husband. Has he been giving you lessons on psychoanalyzing a person?"

She tilted her head, and the firelight illuminated her face. The raised eyebrow and stubborn set of her jaw told him he wouldn't get any peace unless he played along with her.

Ryan sighed. "Okay. Ask your questions."

His sister smiled. "I'll start with something easy. Does Sophia really remind you of me?"

"Definitely. One hundred percent. Wait until you meet her and you'll see if for yourself."

"You've grown quite fond of this little family in the last few days, haven't you?"

Realization of how deep his feelings were for both Sophia and Hadley hit like a bolt of lightning. "Yes." Let his little sister infer whatever she wanted into his answer. He would not elaborate, yet.

She waited a moment but then seemed to accept his one-word answer. Jerking her head toward the motor home, she asked, "Was the camper already decorated when you arrived?"

"Just the lights on the outside."

"So you hung the wreath on the door and set up the small tree on the dinette." She smiled.

"Of course. Hadley wanted it to be festive for Sophia."

"Why was it important to you to build a campfire and make s'mores?"

"I told you, Hadley felt bad that Sophia was missing Christmas at home. It's been hard being on the run the past few days. I thought a campfire and s'mores would cheer them both up temporarily."

"Did you think you'd outsmarted the person chasing you, buying yourselves a little time to catch your breaths and reevaluate how to move forward?"

"Of course! I never would have let Sophia out of my sight if I'd thought she was in danger. I would have locked us all inside the camper. Do you think I'm that insensitive and reckless?"

"No. I don't. Do you?"

He paused, and let her words soak into his brain and every fiber of his body. No. He wasn't reckless. If danger had been evident at that moment, he never would have taken the time to build a campfire and try to provide a little camping experience for Sophia. She'd been so excited that they were going camping, like her favorite cartoon character. All he'd wanted was to help her and her beautiful mother make Christmas memories that didn't involve looking over their shoulders as they ran from an unknown assailant.

"You've gotten very quiet. What are you thinking?" Bridget asked, breaking into his thoughts.

"I'm thinking you're one smart cookie, Peanunchkin." She feigned shock at his use of the nickname he'd made up combining the words *peanut* and *munchkin*, two words she'd hated growing up. He smiled and clasped her hand. "Seriously, as sorry as I am that you and Sawyer are spending your first Christmas as husband and wife helping me track down a kidnapper instead of at home with the family and his sister, I'm so very thankful to have you here keeping me straight." He leaned over and kissed his sister's forehead. "Oh, and message received. While there were a few lapses in my judgment, they weren't made recklessly, and it's not my fault the kidnapper was able to snatch Sophia."

"Great. I'm glad you were able to work that out. Now what is the plan?"

"The plan is to find the kidnapper and get Sophia home for Christmas." He stood and kicked dirt on the campfire, extinguishing its flames. Then he turned and held out his hand to help Bridget out of the low chair. "Let's join the others and come up with a plan. I have a feeling it's going to involve a visit to Misty Hollow Ranch, and I don't mean just to pick up the ransom money."

Ryan couldn't pinpoint exactly how he knew, but he was convinced whoever took Sophia had connections to Carlton McIntyre's ranch. And he intended to get on that ranch as early as possible in the morning to investigate.

When they entered the RV, they found Lincoln and Sawyer hunched together at the small dinette studying the notebook he and Hadley had been writing in. Sawyer looked up and met Ryan's eyes. "I think the kidnapper is someone from Misty Hollow Ranch."

A gasp sounded behind the group, and all eyes turned to see Hadley standing in the doorway to the bedroom. Her hand covered her mouth, and her face was ashen. "But why would anyone there want to hurt me or Sophia? We've been visiting the ranch once a week for the past four months. Plus, we had Thanksgiving at the ranch. If someone from Misty Hollow is responsible for this, why didn't they strike sooner? And why would they ever imagine I'd have that kind of money? Carlton McIntyre is the one with money. Not me."

"We're not saying this is an elaborate plot that involves everyone at the ranch. After talking to Carlton earlier, I can almost guarantee he's not involved. He and his daughter both seemed shocked by the events that occurred tonight." Ryan crossed over to the sofa and sat, then motioned for her to join him. "Come sit down and let's think things through."

After Hadley sat down, he took her hands in his. They were icy cold, so he instantly started rubbing them to increase circulation and add warmth. He could feel three pairs of eyes watching, obvious amusement in them, but he didn't care what Bridge, Sawyer or Linc thought they knew. Hadley had received one shock after the other since arriving home from work on Thursday. He was simply offering comfort in the form of human touch to help her hold her emotions together. *Yeah, right, Vincent. Keep telling yourself that. Maybe you'll start believing it, too.*

"So, how do we proceed? We're supposed to go to the ranch in the morning to get the hundred and fifty thousand dollars for the ransom. We don't even know where the person is keeping Sophia. Do you think she could be on the ranch? And how do we find out?"

Sawyer crossed over to the sitting area and sat in the recliner across from them. Leaning forward, his arms resting on his thighs, he made eye contact with Hadley. Ryan knew his brother-in-law was in full FBI profiler mode. If anyone could help Hadley understand why it was most likely someone from Misty Hollow Ranch was involved, it was Sawyer. "Those are great questions, but unfortunately, we don't have the answers you're seeking. I was basing my prediction off the information in the notes you've been jotting down. It seems like you and Sophia have a fairly strict routine. Other than work and school, you visit your mom for two hours every Saturday, go to the grocery store where you do curbside pickup every Friday—except last week when you went on Thursday—I'm guessing that's because school let out for the holidays on that day…" He paused. After she nodded, he continued, "Church on Sunday for two hours and a midweek Bible class on Wednesday for an hour. You've lived in Eagle Creek for five years, moving there shortly after Sophia was born. I would imagine you've known the people you interact with on a regular basis for as many years, except for the people from Misty Hollow Ranch. Unless…do any of them go to church where you worship?"

"No." Hadley shook her head. "Misty Hollow Ranch is a large spread thirty minutes west of Foster Falls, making it an hour's drive each way. I'm not sure where, if anywhere, the people who live on the ranch worship, but I'd imagine it would be closer to home."

Sawyer sat back in his chair and gave a subtle nod for Ryan to take over the conversation. "I think you can see where Sawyer is going with his line of thinking. Since you are a creature of habit." She visibly balked at his comment, so he rushed on. "That's not an insult, simply a fact. Sticking to a set routine when you're in hiding is a survival technique. It was only natural for you to adopt the habit. By keeping a routine and becoming familiar with the people you'd encounter in each location—church, work, Sophia's school, grocery store—you were training yourself to be able to quickly identify any change in your surroundings. Making it easier for you to sense danger or spot Troy if he suddenly showed up."

"Then four months ago, I changed my routine to include trips to Carlton's ranch. I'm still not sure why the person responsible would wait four months to act, but I see what you're saying. The other people in my life have known us much longer and, most likely, they would have acted sooner." She drew in a deep breath and turned, wide-eyed, toward Ryan. "It's all my fault. I let my guard down and now my baby girl is paying the price."

"No. This isn't your fault. You didn't do anything wrong."

"Yes, I did. I made the mistake of thinking we were safe." Tears welled in her eyes.

He pulled her into his arms and let her cry, vaguely aware of Bridget quietly opening the door and herding the others out of the camper. The door clicked closed, and they were alone. Ryan stroked her hair and murmured soothing words.

A little while later, Hadley pulled away from him. She touched the wet spot on his shirt, where her tears had fallen. "I'm sorry. I didn't mean to soak you."

He shrugged. "No worries. It'll dry."

She looked around the empty motor home. "Where did everyone go?"

"Bridget wanted to give you some privacy, so she and the guys went outside."

"What! It's freezing out there." She started to rise, but he pulled her back down.

"It won't hurt them to stay outside a few minutes longer. First, I need to know you're okay." He searched her face. "Are you?"

"Other than being mortified at my inability to keep my emotions in check, I'm fine."

"Hey." Ryan caught her hand in his and absentmindedly caressed the back of hers with his thumb. "You have every right to cry. Everyone has a different reaction when faced with danger. An emotional response is perfectly acceptable. And while I can't speak from experience, I imagine the emotions you're feeling are intensified since your child is the one in danger."

He placed his free hand on her cheek. "Are you ready for me to have the others rejoin us?"

She bit her lip and nodded, an expression of uncertainty on her face. And like a moth drawn to a flame, he buried his hand in her hair and lowered his head, claiming her lips. Hadley leaned in closer and wrapped her arms around him.

There was a light rap on the door. They jumped apart as Bridget poked her head inside. "Okay if we come back in?" she asked, her eyes taking in the scene.

"Of course." He fought the urge to squirm under his sister's knowing gaze. Ryan knew she'd be full of questions. Fortunately for him, she was a professional, so she'd wait until Sophia was safe in Hadley's arms and the kidnapper had been apprehended before she grilled him.

Which meant he had time to figure out the answers himself, because at the moment he couldn't explain what had come over him. He wanted to pretend it had been an instinctual act of offering comfort through human touch, but that sounded like a flimsy excuse even to himself. No. The kiss had been more than that. Much more. And he knew he'd have to evaluate his actions and feelings at some point in the near future, but not now. Not until he had rescued Sophia.

SEVENTEEN

The knots in Hadley's stomach tightened. She crossed her arms over her abdomen and took a few deep breaths in a vain attempt to ease her nerves. *Lord, I pray the plan we devised last night works. And please, don't let Carlton be involved in Sophia's kidnapping. He's been so kind to us. I'd hate to think his thoughtfulness was part of some sort of ulterior motive.*

"Okay, so let's go over this one more time." She turned sideways in the front passenger seat so she could look into the back, where Bridget and Sawyer sat.

"Hadley, breathe. We kept the plan simple and close enough to the truth that it will be believable." Bridget smiled. "Sawyer and I are newlyweds."

"Fact," Sawyer interjected, leaning in to kiss the top of his wife's head. "We've only been married two months."

"We were snow skiing at Hogadon Basin when

Ryan called to tell us about Sophia's disappearance," Bridget continued. "We rushed to be with you during this ordeal to offer you the support of family."

"Which is mostly true. Ryan is family. He did call. We did rush to be here to offer support," Sawyer said, turning his attention to Hadley. "The only part of the story that's fabricated is the ski vacation, but we have to give a logical explanation for our being here. If we tell them we drove up from Blackberry Falls, Colorado, they're likely to get suspicious about our being here. It's much more logical that we'd travel an hour to be with you than it is that we'd travel eight hours."

"They're already expecting me, so after I've been introduced, I'll make the introductions for Bridget and Sawyer," Ryan said. "You and I will go with Carlton to get the money, and Bridge and Sawyer will wander down to the stables and see if they can find any clues. The main thing for you to remember is to act normal. We may be way off on our assumption. The kidnapper may not be connected to the ranch at all, and everyone you see today may be just as hurt by Sophia's abduction as we are."

Hadley scoffed. "I don't know whether I should pray the kidnapper is or isn't connected to the ranch. I want my child back. Since I walked in and found my home ransacked, this is the first time I've felt hopeful that we were getting closer to answers."

"No matter what we discover at the ranch this morning, we will not give up until we find Sophia. And that includes all of us, not just me," Bridget declared. "If it wasn't before, it is now an official Protective Instincts case. We don't quit until the job is done."

"I can testify to that," Sawyer piped up. "When my sister was held captive by a serial killer last year, I found out just how valuable it was to have Ryan, Linc and Bridget on my side. I've worked with many talented agents in the Bureau through the years, but none of them can compare to the determination and talent of the Protective Instincts team."

"Your sister was abducted?"

"Yes. While I was working on Bridget's grandparents' ranch in Tennessee during a leave of absence from the Bureau. My sister and Bridget were both targeted by a serial killer with a vendetta against me." Sawyer leaned forward in the move Hadley now recognized as his I-want-your-full-attention stance. "So you see, I do understand the emotions and self-doubt you're feeling. The suffocating thought that you didn't do enough to protect a loved one and knowing they're out there somewhere scared and alone waiting for you to reach them will paralyze you—oftentimes at the worst moment possible—if you allow it to."

His words penetrated her mind like no others she'd heard since Sophia was taken. She had to stay strong and be ready to endure whatever blocked her path to her child.

"Also, remember to trust your backup to handle things you can't." He laced his fingers through Bridget's, lifted her hand and kissed the back of it. "If I hadn't trusted Ryan, my sister and Bridget wouldn't be alive."

"Now, honey, I think I was doing a pretty good job of holding my own against Lovelorn when you showed up."

"Is that right?"

"Yes, but of course I was very happy to have Linc and you, my handsome hero, show up to help fight the dastardly villain." Bridget giggled as her husband leaned toward her, wiggling his eyebrows.

Hadley wondered if there would ever come a time that she could look back on this day and laugh. Probably not, but hopefully, she would be able to remember it as the day she and her daughter were reunited.

"Hey. You've got this. Don't overthink things and you'll be fine. Just go in there and treat everyone the same way you always have." Ryan reached across and patted her knee. "I know it's difficult not to worry, but try to remember what Sawyer said—you're not alone on this journey. Just breathe and pray."

Breathe and pray. You aren't Emma Bryant facing an unknown world, all alone and scared. You are Hadley Logan, a child of God. And not only is He walking with you into battle, but you also have these new friends who are ready to stand beside you and fight.

Hadley shifted in her seat so she faced forward, and Ryan's hand slipped off her knee. She instantly missed the connection and regretted the move, although she knew she needed to tread carefully and not let her feelings for Jessica's former fiancé grow any stronger.

The kiss last night had caught her off guard. But if she were being totally honest with herself, the instant his lips had touched hers, she'd been pulled from the almost trancelike daze she'd been in immediately following Sophia's abduction. Until that moment, she'd been functioning on autopilot, becoming so weighted down by the fear of never seeing Sophia again that she'd melted into a puddle of tears.

She realized now that she'd spent much of the past six years simply trying to get by, keeping people and her own emotions at arm's length so she wouldn't run the risk of being hurt physically or emotionally again. After this was all over and Sophia was back home—Hadley refused to believe this would end any other way; doing so would mentally paralyze her, again—she would make sure that she and her daughter became active members of the community.

Hadley would do whatever it took to get her daughter back, and then she'd do her best to allow others into their lives. No more hiding and living in fear. Doing so for all these years hadn't stopped bad things from happening. It had simply limited the number of people who could offer support when needed.

Slowing his speed, Ryan activated his blinker and turned onto the gravel road leading to Misty Hollow Ranch, and stopped. There were miles and miles of fence on either side of the drive enclosing prime pasture land that he imagined was full of cattle in the spring and summer months.

"How far to the house?" Ryan asked, peering at the gravel driveway that stretched out before them. "The road seems to disappear at the horizon."

"I had the same thought on my first visit here," she said. "The drive is about two miles long. There's a curve right before we reach a grove of trees. As soon as you drive through them, there's a clearing and then you'll see the house, which is nestled against a mountain. Be prepared to be wowed, though. This is the most spectacular home I've ever seen."

His biological mother had died when he was ten, and George Vincent—who coached the little league baseball team that both his son Nate and Ryan played on and who knew Ryan had no other family—had taken him home with him and announced it was his new home. The 4,000-square-feet log home had seemed like a mansion. Then he'd stepped through the doors and seen the brightly colored throw pillows, family photos and knickknacks. A homey feeling had settled over him and he'd soon realized that the only thing that made his new family's home different from the small two-bedroom apartment he'd spent ten years of his life in with his mom was the size. The artwork on the walls might be worth thousands of dollars whereas the ones in his childhood home were his own finger-painted masterpieces, but the warm, cozy vibe and the feeling of home were the same.

He pulled up to the wooden archway that stood thirty feet off the road, a cast-iron sign hanging from above proudly announcing the name MISTY HOLLOW RANCH. The sun peeked from behind an ominous snow cloud and a glint of light bounced off the sign, catching his attention. A hidden camera was tucked discreetly inside the intricately scrolled ironwork. Though he'd known they needed to bring Hadley along for the cash, he'd been hesitant to come to this location not knowing anything about the people on the ranch, but this was a promising start. If Carlton McIntyre was cautious enough to have a camera hidden at the entrance of his property line and not just close to his home, it gave Ryan hope that the security on the ranch would be up to his standards. And hopefully, he'd be able to gain access to the footage that had been recorded over the past few days—either via access granted by Carlton himself or through his own, less than aboveboard means. He preferred the former, but when a child's life was in danger, he would use any means at his disposal. Lincoln was already sitting in his SUV at a service station a mile up the road, with Ryan's laptop and surveillance equipment.

Ryan put the vehicle into Park and turned to peer into the back. "There are surveillance cameras. I need to know make and model if at all possible. If there is a security team watching the live footage, I'm sure they'd see us if Hadley or I tried to get a photo. Sawyer, see if you can zoom in far enough with your phone camera to get a couple of good photos. We'll send them to Linc so he can try and find a workaround if needed to get access to the footage. Bridge, is Linc in place and can we hear him?"

"Yes. And the signal is strong." She leaned forward and handed him a discrete earpiece that matched the ones both she and Sawyer were wearing.

"Good." He inserted the audio device into his ear that was turned away from the prying lens of the surveillance camera. "Linc, can you hear me?"

"Loud and clear."

"There are surveillance cameras at the gate, so we'll have to be careful from this point on. Sawyer is going to send you some photos. Try and match the make and model. The information will be important if we need to hack into the system."

"Got it!"

Sawyer settled back against his seat and scrolled through the images. "Sending them now."

Ryan heard a ping over the earpiece. "Linc, those should be the photos of the surveillance cameras. Start with an image search and see if you can find a close match."

"Got it. And guys—" Linc's voice took on a serious note "—be careful. You don't know who you can and can't trust in there."

"We'll proceed with caution," Sawyer answered before Ryan could. "And my friends from the Bureau are sticking close to the area. I didn't tell them we suspect the kidnapper is connected to the ranch because it's just a theory and we don't have any proof. But they know Carlton is putting up the money for the ransom, so they are staying nearby in case something happens."

"Yeah, I already spotted them." Linc laughed. "When this is over, maybe we need to give your friends tips on how to blend in when they're trying to be incognito."

"You're probably right," Sawyer replied. "I've never seen any group of people as adept at changing their appearance or blending in as you three."

"You know, it's slightly unsettling having you three involved in a conversation that I only hear one side of," Hadley said, her gaze fixed on the trio.

"I'm sorry. I wish I could give you an earpiece, but if you're not used to wearing one, it can be unnerving and we can't have you startled at a crucial moment. It could blow our cover." Ryan shifted into Drive. "Okay, gang, let's do this."

A cloud of dust billowed out behind his vehicle as they made their way to the homestead. The occupants would have been alerted to their arrival even without the added security of the camera. The fields were nice and flat and the eye could easily travel for a half mile. They drew near a wooded area and, just as Hadley had stated, once they drove into the clearing, he saw a massive two-story log and rock Western-style mansion. Easily 6,000-square-feet. It was indeed impressive. Tucked back in a secluded area of the ranch with a mountain backdrop, it was breathtaking. But even more important than the beautiful home in the equally beautiful setting was the ten-foot-tall black iron fence surrounding the homestead. Security cameras, encased in black to match the fence, were mounted discreetly above the gate. So far, Carlton's bragging that he could protect Hadley and Sophia seemed to have merit. Had Ryan put Sophia in danger by not trusting someone else to help protect her? No. He knew, deep inside his gut, that the kidnapper had connections to this place, and no matter how well guarded it was, they would have still found a way to take Sophia.

Now it was up to him to get her back. He could not fail. Not just for Hadley's sake, but for his own, too. No matter how determined he'd been not to bond with Troy's child, he had. And he couldn't imagine loving her more if she were his own.

And her beautiful mother. *Lord, I love them. Both of them. I don't know if they can accept me into their lives, but whether they do or not, I can't lose Sophia this way. Please, guide me and give me a clear mind to look at the evidence so I can find her and reunite her with her mom.*

* * *

Anxiety and fear engulfed Hadley; her body zinged like she had touched a live wire on an electric fence. Could the others feel the panic radiating off her? She prayed they couldn't. Crossing her arms over her midsection, she held herself tightly, as if doing so could keep her emotions from crumbling into a thousand tiny pieces.

"Hey," Ryan said softly so only she could hear. "It's going to be okay. I won't let anything happen to you."

"I'm not worried about me." She swallowed the lump in her throat. "Just find my daughter."

"We will." He pulled to a stop in front of the house, then turned and faced her. "Remember, act naturally. There's no reason to suspect Carlton or his immediate household to be involved in this. Most likely, it's someone new to the ranch. Otherwise, why wait four months to act?"

She nodded.

There was a knock on the passenger-side window and she jumped. "Y'all come on out of there. We've been waiting for you." Carlton peered at her, his eyes going from Hadley to Ryan and back again.

Mikael stood several feet behind her father, a frown on her face. Was she still upset that he'd agreed to put up the ransom money? Hadley couldn't say she blamed the older woman.

One hundred and fifty thousand dollars was a lot of money, but she would pay it back, even if it took her the rest of her life.

Hadley stepped out of the SUV and Carlton immediately swept her into a bear hug. Instantly, she knew without a doubt, for whatever reason, this man loved her and Sophia. There was no way he was involved in the kidnapping.

She returned the friendly gesture. Warmth engulfed her, replacing the icy fear that had run through her veins moments earlier. "Thank you," she whispered. "I promise I'll repay—"

"Shhh. Don't worry about that. First things first." He pulled back and searched her face. "You and your young man come inside, and we'll talk in private."

Ryan came up beside her and held out his hand to Carlton. "Hello, sir. I'm Ryan. I hope you don't mind, but my sister, Bridget, and her husband, Sawyer, are with us." He turned as Bridget and Sawyer piled out of the SUV. "They were skiing at Hogadon Basin when they heard about Sophia and immediately came to show their support and be here for Hadley."

"I don't mind at all." Carlton raised a brow, but if he questioned Ryan's story, he didn't say anything. "However, maybe they can wait in the great room while we discuss matters in my study."

"If it's okay, could we stretch our legs before coming inside?" Bridget asked, with a look of wide-eyed innocence.

"Now, honey," Sawyer interjected. "People don't want strangers wandering around their property."

"Oh, no. I don't mind at all. That will give me a chance to talk to Hadley in private."

Hadley instantly reached for Ryan's hand. Even though she felt in her heart that Carlton wasn't involved in any of this, there was no way she was going to face him or anyone else on this ranch alone. "Stay with me," she pleaded.

He smiled. "I'm not going anywhere."

Then she turned back to Carlton. "Ryan's been my rock this entire time. He might be able to fill you in on details that my mind is fuzzy about."

"Of course." Carlton motioned for them to follow him. "Mikael, show our guests the stables. They might appreciate seeing our Thoroughbreds, and it will be a bit warmer than waiting outside."

"But Dad, I wanted to—"

He pinned his daughter with a look that silenced her, then he went inside expecting Hadley and Ryan to be right behind him.

Hadley had never seen an exchange like that between father and daughter before. They'd always been very loving and respectful toward each other. Had her request for the loan put a strain on their relationship? Mikael probably thought it was bold of Hadley to come to her dad for money; after all, it wasn't like she and Sophia were relatives coming to family members when in need.

"Mikael, I'm sorry. I have no right to put you both in the middle of this." Hadley's steps faltered. "If I had another option, I'd take it. But I know you're fond of Sophia, too."

"You're right. I love her like she's my own. And I'm okay doing whatever it takes to get her home." The older woman turned and headed toward the stables.

Bridget scurried to keep up with Mikael. "This ranch is huge. I bet it takes a lot of people to run a place like this. How many cowboys will we get to see?"

Sawyer looked at Bridget and smiled. "Now, honey, don't you go mooning over any cowboys. Don't forget you're a married woman."

"Is that part of the act?" Hadley lowered her voice and whispered to Ryan.

"My sister has a way of making people talk." Ryan placed his hand on Hadley's lower back and stayed glued to her side as they entered the house.

In spite of the security his presence gave her, a chill snaked up her spine the moment she crossed the threshold. She searched for unknown evil lurking in the shadows of the rooms that she had once thought were so welcoming. But now, even the bright holiday decorations couldn't chase away the fear brought on by the negative vibe.

Stop it. You are safe here. Carlton and Mikael are the same people who welcomed you into their home and provided Sophia with riding lessons, giving her a somewhat normal childhood that you couldn't provide. If someone at Misty Hollow Ranch is involved in Sophia's disappearance, it's an employee, not them.

Hadley trembled. Ryan must have sensed she was allowing her fear to take over. He slid his hand from her back to her waist, drew her close and kissed her temple. "It's okay. I'm right here," he murmured in her ear.

Carlton stopped outside the door to his study, turned and raised an eyebrow, a quizzical expression on his face as he viewed the scene. Good. Let him think they were more than friends. It would help with the cover and provide an excuse for them to be inseparable.

"So you two are close *friends*?" Carlton locked eyes with Ryan. "It's surprising, Hadley has never mentioned you. We've had many long talks. She's always said she wasn't interested in dating anyone. Sophia is her priority."

Hadley opened her mouth but Ryan answered

before she could. "As it should be. I love what a doting mother she is to Sophia."

"How long have you known each other?"

"Oh, Hadley's known me for years, but we just recently reconnected." He turned to her. "When was it you first saw me across the room? Six... six and a half years ago?"

She appreciated what he was doing, wording things in a manner so she could answer without telling a lie. When had she first seen him, or rather pictures of him in the collage of photos on the wall behind the sofa in Jessica's apartment?

"Six and a half years." Her response sounded forced, even to her own ears. She cleared her throat. "The first thing I noticed about you were your blue eyes. Probably because your u—"

"I'd forgotten I was wearing a blue suit," Ryan interrupted her, his gaze warning her to not over-share details.

Acting normal when you weren't sure if the people you'd thought of as friends might in reality be enemies was much harder than she'd ever imagined. *Please, Lord, don't let me be mistaken about Carlton being a good person. If I have misjudged him, I'm not sure I'll ever be able to trust my instincts ever again.*

EIGHTEEN

Once they were in Carlton's study, behind closed doors, Ryan turned to the older gentleman. "Hadley said you've been a surrogate grandfather to her and Sophia. I don't mind answering any of your questions, once Sophia is found and safe."

"Of course, most of my questions can wait. But I'm sure you understand. I have a few that need answering before I hand over such a large sum of money."

Hadley stiffened beside him, but Ryan smiled. "I would expect nothing less from an astute businessman like yourself. One who's built one of the largest cattle ranches in the western United States."

The old cowboy, dressed in faded jeans and well-worn boots, squared his shoulders and narrowed his eyes. "Seems like you've done some diggin' into my background. You have me at a disadvantage. Without your last name, I wasn't able to do the same. So, why don't you fill me in on who you really are and what you're doing here."

"I'm someone who cares deeply for Hadley and Sophia, and who wants to find that little girl and reunite her with her mother." He held Carlton's gaze, refusing to blink. There was true concern in the older gentleman's eyes.

Ryan understood. Carlton probably thought he was involved in the abduction somehow and had coerced Hadley to give him the money, like a con artist preying on an innocent victim. It was obvious Carlton loved Hadley and Sophia. Though that just brought more questions to the forefront of Ryan's mind.

Right now, his only focus was finding Sophia and keeping Hadley safe. Ryan turned to Hadley. "Give me a minute to talk privately with Carlton."

"She can wait in the living room. Then we can have more privacy." Carlton spoke up.

"No. She stays where I can see her and protect her," Ryan answered without looking at the man.

Hadley nodded and did as he requested, sitting in an oversize chair in what appeared to be a reading corner of the study. Ryan gave her a soft kiss on the forehead. "Trust me," he whispered. "It's going to be okay."

She smiled and folded her hands in her lap, her

cell phone clasped tightly in one, as she waited for the next text from the kidnapper. He knew that with each passing minute, her dread that it might never arrive rose also.

Turning back to their host, he gave a slight jerk of his head, indicating they should stand by the large mahogany desk set back against a wall of bookshelves. Carlton nodded and made his way behind the desk, sitting with his hand on his right thigh, his fingers brushing the drawer that Ryan had no doubt held a gun. If the situation weren't so serious, Ryan would burst out laughing at the Old West scene that played out before him.

"I understand and appreciate your distrust of me. That simply means we're on the same side. You love these girls as much as I do." Ryan turned sideways so Carlton could watch him reach into his back pocket. "I'm going to withdraw my wallet so I can give you some identification."

Using two fingers, Ryan extracted the leather wallet his adoptive mother had given him on his eleventh birthday. Mocha-colored leather with his initials RJV branded on it. Inside there had been three photos, one of his biological mother, one of his new adoptive parents, and one of his new siblings Charlie, Nate, Bridget, Hoyt and Ethan. Twenty years later, the leather was a little worn, but it was still his favorite wallet. When she gave it to him, she had told him she wasn't trying to replace his biological mom, but she wanted him to know he was a Vincent now. And that meant, whether he wanted her to worry about him or not or even love him or not didn't matter, because she would and she did. That night, seven months after he'd walked into her home, she became his mom. And he'd finally softened around the edges enough to welcome the rest of the family into his heart.

Dropping the wallet onto the desk, Ryan said, "Go ahead. Search through it. I don't have anything to hide."

Carlton picked the wallet up, flipped it open and examined the driver's license that was tucked behind the clear plastic protective sleeve. "Ryan James Vincent. Blackberry Falls, Colorado." The older man's head jerked upward, one eyebrow cocked. "Any relation to George Vincent?"

"Yes, sir. He's my dad."

"George and I have crossed paths several times through the years at various horse shows. Although, we're not much more than acquaintances, he has always struck me as being a fair, honest man."

Riffling through the other contents, Carlton withdrew Ryan's business card. "Protective Instincts, Inc. Private security firm. Ryan Vincent co-owner." He waved the business card at Ryan. "Private security firm. And you want me to believe you just happened to wander back into my da—Hadley's life at this exact moment?"

"I had a specific purpose for coming into Hadley's life. However, my reason had nothing to do with the attack on her in her home." Ryan prayed he was right. Though he knew they hadn't been able to find anything to connect Troy's family to the attacks, a small part of him still wondered if... No. His brother-in-law had the best instincts of anyone he knew, and if Sawyer felt Hadley's connection to the kidnapper had something to do with Misty Hollow Ranch, then Ryan knew he was on the right track. "I am just thankful I was there. And now I am determined to do whatever necessary to get Sophia back. Are you going to help, or not?"

There was a long pause, but then Carlton turned to the bookcase behind his desk, his back blocking Ryan's view. There was a soft click and the bookcase slid, revealing a hidden wall safe. He punched in a series of numbers and then pulled the safe door open. Carlton peered into the safe. "What?" He reached in and moved some papers and small boxes. "It's gone. My money is gone!"

Mikael burst into the room and he turned to her. "Mikael, where's my emergency cash?"

"I tried to tell you last night." She shook her head, an exasperated expression on her face. "Don't have time right now."

"Tell. Me. Now," Carlton said through clenched teeth.

"Can't. We have an emergency. Tank is loose. He charged at Bridget and Sawyer, and now they're trapped in a stall."

"Who didn't latch his pen correctly?" Carlton growled.

"Who or what is Tank?" Ryan asked.

"A fifty-thousand-dollar Angus bull," Mikael said over her shoulder, then turned back to her dad. "He keeps ramming the stall door. And neither Gus nor I can get close enough to wrangle him back into his pen. He's either going to injure himself or, worse, break through the door and kill your guests."

"I'll get the tranquilizer gun." Carlton marched over to the gun safe sitting against one wall and quickly entered the combination and spun the dial to open it. Reaching in, he removed a long-barrel gun.

Carlton glanced at Hadley, who'd jumped up from her chair when Mikael burst into the room. "I'll be back as quickly as I can and we'll get the money situation straightened out." He turned back to his daughter and added, between clenched teeth, "And you have some explaining to do."

"Yes, sir, but first can we take care of the situation at hand?"

"Let's go," the old cowboy responded.

"If my sister's in danger, I'm coming with you." Ryan took two steps toward the door, then stopped and turned, Hadley on his heels. "No. You can't go. We don't know if—" He swallowed the remainder of his words and looked around the room.

"You think the person responsible for taking Sophia is someone on my ranch?" Realization dawned on Carlton's face. "Do you think this was set up to lure Hadley out into the open?"

"Trap or not, we have two people whose lives are in immediate danger. Unless we take care of Tank, now!" Mikael insisted.

"She's right. I've got to go. You two. Stay here," Carlton said.

"I'll stay here." Hadley grasped Ryan's arms and turned him toward the door. "Go. I know you're worried about Bridget and Sawyer."

"Are you sure?" He was torn. Ryan needed to make sure his *baby* sister was okay. He'd never forgive himself if something happened to her because he'd pulled her and Sawyer away from their original Christmas plans to help him protect Hadley. But he'd also never forgive himself if Hadley was hurt because he was distracted. "No. I can't."

"Yes, you can. I'll lock the door. No one will be able to get inside."

"But—"

"She's right," Mikael interrupted. "Either way, come or stay. Doesn't matter to me, but we've gotta go before Tank breaks through that stall and your sister and her husband are unrecognizable."

"Go." Hadley pushed him gently on his back.

"Okay, but lock the door. And don't open it until you hear my voice. Got it?" Ryan turned and raced out the door, pausing just long enough to hear the click of the lock. He prayed she took his instructions seriously and stayed locked inside until his return.

Hadley paced back and forth in rhythm to the ticking of the old mantel clock that sat on the chunky wooden beam above the stone fireplace. She'd been in Carlton's study on numerous occasions, drinking coffee and having long chats while Sophia was outside in the corral having a riding lesson with Mikael. Hadley had watched the first few lessons, but Sophia had seemed distracted by her presence, always looking to make sure her mother had seen her when she'd done something correctly. Carlton had eventually convinced her that Sophia would make better progress and run less risk of falling off and getting hurt if she were out of sight.

She had eventually allowed him and his housekeeper, Mrs. Emerson, to coax her indoors with coffee and pastries. The riding lessons usually lasted an hour. During that time, Hadley had fallen into the habit of either reading one of Carlton's many books sitting in the leather chair in front of the fireplace in his study or learning to bake in the kitchen with Joyce. Other than her home, the ranch had become the place where she felt safest. The people here were like family to her. She could not imagine any of them wanting to harm her. Or Sophia.

She sank onto the leather chair, where a week ago she'd read the first two chapters of a first-edition copy of *Oliver Twist,* and covered her face with her hands. What had happened to the money Carlton had promised to loan her to use for the ransom? It was obvious he had been shocked when he opened the safe and saw it was missing? Hadley had no idea what she was going to do now.

Her cell phone pinged. An image of a map with detailed directions, followed by a text message from the kidnapper.

Nice to see you at the ranch this morning. Time's up! Follow the map and bring the money to the old mine. Come alone! If I see your boyfriend or anyone else with you, you'll never see your daughter again. You have fifteen minutes... Time starts now.

Fifteen minutes! Hadley jumped to her feet, knocking over the armchair in the process. She darted toward the door and skidded to a stop. Money. She needed money. They wouldn't let her have Sophia if she came empty-handed.

She thought of the escape-plan money she'd been hoarding away for an emergency. She had packed it in her backpack at the start of the trip. Granted there was only twenty-seven thousand dollars, not nearly the one hundred and fifty thousand the kidnapper had demanded, but it was all she had. She'd take the backpack with clothes and things stuffed in the bottom and stack the money on top. Hopefully, they would look inside, see the money and think it was all there. If they decided to count the money, maybe she could grab Sophia and run.

Tick. Tick. Tick. The sound of the mantel clock seemed to increase in volume with each second that passed. A reminder that time was running out.

She opened the door and peeked into the hall.

No one was in sight. *Hurry. Hurry. Hurry.* Her mind echoed in the same cadence as the mantel clock.

Her heart pounding in her chest, she raced down the hall and through the front door, not stopping until she reached the SUV. Loud shouts and the sound of people scurrying indicated the others were still busy trying to corral the prized bull.

Reaching into the front seat, she grabbed the backpack that held the money and Sophia's and her passports from the floorboard. She opened it, removed both passports and tucked them into the inner pocket of her winter coat. Then she reached into the bottom of the bag and pulled out the money and spread it out over the top of the other items inside. Cinching the drawstring, she closed the flap over the top and snapped it closed. Then she slid her arms through the straps and fastened the pack onto her back. Now, how was she going to make it to the designated location?

Carlton kept an ATV parked behind the main house. The key hung on a hook in the kitchen. She turned and ran smack into Mikael.

"Whoa. Where are you going?" Carlton's daughter caught Hadley and held her upright.

"Oh, um. Nowhere. Just needed to check something." She couldn't tell the other woman where she was going. *If I see your boyfriend or anyone else with you, you'll never see your daughter again.*

Was the kidnapper implying he'd kill Sophia if Hadley didn't follow his instructions to a T? She had to convince Mikael everything was okay and she was returning to Carlton's study, or she might run to Ryan and Carlton and tell them she was headed to meet the kidnapper.

"I don't believe you. You're wearing a backpack and acting suspicious. The kidnapper contacted you again." Mikael leaned in and searched her face. "Are you really going to go meet them alone? I didn't think you'd be that brave."

Anger and frustration bubbled up inside her, and she squared her shoulders. "You have absolutely no clue how brave I can be. I will do anything to protect my daughter. Now, get out of my way. I have someplace to be. And less than ten minutes to get there before it's too late." Using her shoulder to brush past the older woman, she headed toward the house.

Mikael grasped her upper arm, her fingers biting into her flesh. "You're not going alone. I'll go with you."

"No!" she said. Her voice rang out like a starting pistol at a racetrack, and Hadley prayed no one in the stables had heard her. She lowered her voice. "I have to go alone or they will kill Sophia."

The other woman's face blanched. "They said that?"

"Not in so many words, but they did tell me I'd never see her again if I didn't come alone."

"So we won't let them see me. I'll stay out of sight, but I'll be there if backup is needed." Mikael half dragged her to an old, beat-up farm truck. She opened the door and turned to her. "Keys are in it. You drive. I'll hide under the tarp in the back."

Hadley pulled free and stood her ground. "No. We can't take the risk."

"Fine. Find your own way there." Mikael leaned into the truck and placed her hand over the horn. "And the second you step away from the truck, I'll blow the horn and start yelling. Everyone will come running."

"Why would you do that?"

"Because, one way or the other, I'm going alone."

"And what are you going to do if the kidnapper has a gun and he sees you?"

Mikael reached behind the seat and extracted a rifle. "I never go into the woods unprotected."

"Then let me take the gun and go alone. Why put yourself in danger, too?"

A smile lifted the corner of Mikael's mouth.

"You and Sophia have become family. I'm going to take care of both of you." She stepped back and motioned for Hadley to get inside the truck. "Are we going? Or will you risk the kidnapper harming your daughter?"

"Fine. But please, stay out of sight unless you think we're in danger." Hadley slid behind the wheel, thankful the truck, though old, was an automatic and not a manual transmission. "And, Mikael…"

"Yeah?"

"Thank you. I would have, as I've done before, faced whatever danger was thrown my way to protect my daughter on my own. But it's nice to know I have people who care in my corner, and I no longer have to face dangers alone."

Mikael didn't say a word. With the rifle still gripped in her hand, she closed the door, climbed into the bed of the truck, lay down and covered herself with the tarp as promised. Thankfully, Carlton had spent an afternoon a couple of weeks ago showing her and Sophia around, giving her the advantage of knowing where the dirt road was that led to the back of the property. And although they hadn't gone near the old gold mine, he'd mentioned in passing that they should never go to that area of the ranch alone because of the dangers of falling down a shaft.

Hadley started the vehicle and headed down

the driveway. Once she rounded the curve out of sight of the house, she'd take the narrow dirt road trail that ran through the woods along the fence line and led to various areas on the seventeen-hundred-acre ranch.

Dear Lord, please keep Sophia safe and don't let harm come to Mikael for putting her own life on the line to help me.

NINETEEN

"I'm sorry about that, folks." Carlton pulled out a bandanna and wiped the sweat off his brow. "I don't know how Tank ended up in the horse stables. We always keep him in the barn in the winter months, but never in the same location as the horses. But I promise, I'll get to the bottom of it. Someone will answer for their carelessness."

"Before you do that, we need to get back to Hadley. I left her alone way longer than I'd planned. The kidnapper should be messaging her any minute, and we need to figure out the money situation." Ryan looked to his sister and brother-in-law. "You two might as well come with us."

"Glad everyone's okay." Linc's voice sounded across their earpieces. None of them acknowledged his comment, knowing he didn't expect them to and doing so would let Carlton know his home was under surveillance.

They stepped out of the stables as an old, blue-and-white pickup truck rounded the house in the opposite direction. "Who's in the truck?" Ryan asked.

"That's Mikael's farm truck. She uses it mainly to check and repair downed fence lines." Carlton furrowed his brow. "We finished our fence repairs in mid-November. Not sure why she'd be headed out that way unless one of the neighbors called and needed her help."

"I didn't see her on her phone, did you?"

"No, but we were slightly busy trying to save your kin," the older man replied. "If you think it might be important, I'll call her to see what's going on after we get back to the study and check on Hadley."

A sinking feeling settled in Ryan's gut. *Please, let Hadley be safe. Please. I never should have left her alone.* He took off at a full sprint, Bridget and Sawyer at his heels.

Barging through the front door, they raced down the hall. Ryan's heart skipped a beat when he saw the door to Carlton's study standing open. His hand automatically went to his gun, tucked into its holster in his waistband at his back. Bridget and Sawyer drew their guns, too, and flanked the sides of the opening. Sawyer nodded for Ryan to enter first, and they would follow.

Ryan knew what he would find before he even stepped inside the room. Hadley was gone. The trio holstered their weapons as Carlton entered the study, his age and new hip slowing his progress.

"What's going on here?" the older man demanded.

"That's what we want to know." Ryan turned on their host. "Where has your daughter gone? Is she behind the kidnapping?"

"You're being ridiculous. Why would Mikael have any reason to kidnap her niece or to harm her sister?"

"Her niece and sister? Are you telling me Hadley is your daughter?"

Carlton's face paled. He sank onto the nearest chair. "I had planned to tell her tomorrow after Christmas dinner, but… Do you think she knows?"

Puffing out a breath, Ryan raked his hand through his hair. "No. Or, at least, I don't think so. But why haven't you told her before now? You've had twenty-eight years."

"I didn't even know she existed until I met her at the nursing home four months ago. She looks so much like her mother at that age, except with my hair and eye color. Sadly, when Hadley introduced me to her mom, Donna didn't remember me." The older gentleman frowned. "Alzheimer's is a tragic illness."

"There are a lot of people with blond hair and

hazel eyes. How do can you be sure Hadley isn't someone else's daughter?"

"If her looks weren't enough to convince me, her name was. Hadley was my grandmother's name. Donna knew that, and I believe it was her way of honoring this side of our daughter's family." Carlton sighed. "I hired Donna to be a nanny to my son, C.J., after my wife died in childbirth. C.J. died at age eight months due to an undiagnosed heart defect. That night after Mikael went to sleep, I found Donna sitting in the nursery crying in the dark. We were both hurting, and I wanted to console her. Only a hug soon turned to a kiss and… The next morning when I woke up I discovered Donna had left in the middle of the night, not even staying for C.J.'s funeral."

"You didn't look for her?"

"No. I was double her age. Besides, it was obvious she regretted what had happened between us." Carlton met Ryan's gaze. "Because of the Alzheimer's, I'll never know why she didn't tell me about Hadley. Even if she didn't want a life with me, I could have helped financially, and Mikael and I could have been part of Hadley's life."

He sat on the chair opposite Carlton and leaned forward, his elbows on his knees. "Does Mikael know Hadley is her sister?"

"Yes. I told her two weeks ago. I didn't want her to be shocked when I told Hadley." A fleeting sadness crossed his face, but then he shook his head and shuttered his expression. "You can't seriously think that Mikael is behind this? She loves Sophia. I've seen the way they interact. She would never harm that little girl. Or Hadley. She might not like the circumstances of Hadley's birth, but Mikael is loyal to family."

A hand on his arm halted Ryan's response. He looked up into his sister's face. Bridget gave a slight shake of her head and mouthed, "We're wasting time."

Sawyer, who had been hanging back, came to stand beside Ryan. "Mr. McIntyre, no one is questioning your daughter's loyalty to family. However, Hadley is missing, and Mikael's the only person we've seen leaving the area. Ryan's business partner and two FBI agents are on standby a few miles down the road."

"You brought agents here? Were you trying to trap my daughter?"

"No, sir. I'm a former FBI agent who currently works as a contracted employee on occasion. When we heard of Sophia's abduction, I immediately contacted the Bureau for help instead of waiting for local authorities to do so," Sawyer said in a calming voice like one would use on a frightened adolescent. "The agents are here to be on hand when we get the call to make the money drop. That's all."

Sawyer was in full FBI profiler mode, and Ryan was thankful for his presence.

"Hey, guys." Linc's voice sounded over the earpieces. "I relocated to have a clear view of the driveway onto the property, and no vehicles have left the ranch. That means, unless there's a second exit we aren't aware of, Hadley still has to be on the property."

"Is there another way in and out of this property?" Enough time had been wasted. Ryan jumped out of his seat. With or without the older man's permission, he was going to search every corner of the property for Hadley. "Carlton, answer me."

Bridget brushed past him and knelt beside the old cowboy. "Mr. McIntyre. Whether Mikael is behind Sophia and Hadley's disappearances or she's innocent and has run off trying to protect them, I don't know. What I do know is you have two daughters and a granddaughter who are missing. Our partner hasn't seen anyone leave the property. This means Hadley and Mikael are still on your land or they took another exit." She placed her hand on Carlton's arm. "Please, help us. We'll find them and do our best to bring them all back here safely. Then we can sort everything out."

A tear slid down the old man's weathered cheek and he patted Bridget's hand. "We'll have to split up. I'll draw you a map of the property and get some of my men to help us search. There's a lot of land to cover."

With a sigh, Carlton pushed to his feet and crossed to his desk, Bridget, Sawyer and Ryan close behind. Reaching into a filing cabinet drawer, he pulled out a copy of the land survey of his property. Then he turned to his printer and scanned a copy of the document. Sitting in his desk chair, he picked up a red fine-tip felt pen and started to draw a line on the map. "Considering the direction Mikael went when she left out of here a few minutes ago, this would be the only road she could take if she didn't go out to the main highway. It forms a Y here." He drew an angled line to the right. "This road goes up the side of the mountain and ends at an old abandoned mine shaft. Whereas this one—" a longer red mark formed the left angled line of the Y "—leads to a hunting cabin."

Carlton capped the pen, dropped it onto the desk and snatched up the map. Then he turned to the trio and held out the map to Bridget. "You and Sawyer check out the hunting cabin. Ryan and I will check out the old mine. While we do that, I'll have my men canvass the property on horseback."

Their host pulled out his cell phone, punched in a number and then quickly gave orders for his men to saddle horses. Disconnecting the call, Carlton crossed to his gun safe and withdrew a rifle and ammo. "In case we run into coyotes or other predators," he asserted.

It sounded like the old cowboy was trying to convince himself, more than anyone else in the room, that the only dangers on his ranch were the wild animals and not his oldest daughter.

"Will we be on horseback, too?" Ryan asked.

"You and I will be. Since the hunting cabin is farther away, Sawyer and Bridget can take my snowmobile." Without looking back, Carlton led them out of his study and down the hall toward the back of the house, his stride longer and swifter than it had been moments before. Urgency and adrenaline were most likely fueling his movements.

Ryan knew the man was eager to find Mikael and prove she wasn't involved in Sophia's kidnapping and Hadley's disappearance. He hoped, for Hadley's sake, Carlton was correct and his oldest daughter was innocent.

White knuckled, Hadley gripped the steering wheel as the truck bounced along over the old rutted trail. There was a rap on the back window and she glanced over her shoulder. Mikael motioned for her to open the sliding rear window. Frustration boiled. The older woman had promised to stay hidden. Hadley pressed on the brake—a little too hard—and Mikael slammed against the cab.

She put the gearshift into Park, turned and opened the small window. "Sorry about that. What'd you want?"

Mikael leaned back, resting on her legs, and scowled at Hadley. "I want you to slow down. I'm tired of being slung around back here."

"I told you not to come." Hadley pressed on the gas, and Mikael toppled backward. "Sorry!" she yelled over her shoulder. "But I only have three minutes to reach the old mine before time's up."

Mikael pulled herself to her knees and poked her head through the window opening. "The mine is over that next ridge. Now, slow down and let me get covered with the tarp," she demanded harshly.

Puffing out a breath, Hadley eased her foot off the accelerator and allowed the truck to slow. She couldn't blame Mikael for being upset. She wouldn't want to be the one in the back of the pickup truck. Fear and anxiety had driven her to charge along this trail at breakneck speed. If Hadley didn't get her emotions in check and make her decisions rationally, she would jeopardize not only her own and Sophia's lives but also Mikael's. A quick glance at the rearview mirror showed the older woman pulling the tarp over her body. Once this was over, if they got out of here alive, she owed Mikael an apology. She hadn't asked to get dragged into Hadley's problems and had only insisted on coming along because she thought she could protect her and help get Sophia back.

For six years, Hadley had kept people at a distance, not believing there was anyone she could call on for help. Until now. The image of Ryan rushing to her aid the first day he showed up in her life flashed in her mind. He had stood before her with a look of determination on his handsome face and piercing blue eyes that showed confidence and concern at the same time.

Lord, if anything happens to me and... Tears burned the backs of her eyes. She sucked in a deep breath and pushed the thought of Sophia not making it back alive out of her mind. *Just, please don't let Ryan blame himself. He's spent too many years feeling remorse over not being able to protect Jessica, though we both know that wasn't his fault. It's time he moves on, finds a wife and has the family he deserves.*

Over the past few days, she'd come to depend on Ryan's strength and protection, and when he shared tender moments with her daughter, she had even caught herself daydreaming of a future with him. Realistically, Hadley knew once this entire situation was settled—whether she got out alive and Sophia's kidnapper was captured or not—he would go back to his life in Denver, and they'd probably never cross paths again.

Topping the ridge, she pressed the brake and surveyed the land around her. A curvier trail wound down the other side of the mountain and led to two decaying cabins beside a creek that wove through the small valley. Fifty yards behind the shacks appeared to be the mine entrance. Now boarded up and covered with wild vegetation and vines. There was a solitary horse tied to a small tree beside one of the cabins, but there wasn't any sign of a person.

"What are you waiting for?" Mikael's muffled voice came through the open window. "Get down there so I can confront the person who demanded a ransom."

"Just stay hidden until we're sure Sophia is safe. We don't want him hurting her because you showed up, too." Hadley took her foot off the brake and started the descent.

As she neared the cabin where the horse stood, the front door swung open and a man with red hair and a mustache stepped outside with a shotgun in his hands. Desmond. The ranch hand who took care of the horses. Her heart dropped. He was also the son of the foreman. Did this mean Sophia's kidnapping involved multiple employees on Carlton's ranch?

No. She shook her head, that couldn't be the case. Surely, if there were more than one person involved, they couldn't have pulled off something so horrific without Carlton—or at least Mikael—noticing or overhearing something. That meant he had to be working alone. Right? Hope soared inside her. Sophia could be inside the cabin.

Taking a deep breath, she exhaled and pushed her jagged nerves out with the breath. *You're not alone. You have Mikael. She's here to protect you and help get Sophia back.*

Leaving the engine running in case they needed to make a quick escape, Hadley put the truck into Park and opened her door. She put her hands up, palms forward, and stepped out of the vehicle. "Where's Sophia?"

"You ain't the one asking questions here. I am." He lifted the shotgun to his shoulder and pointed the barrel at her. "How come you're in Mikael's truck?"

"I didn't have my vehicle. It was this or walk."

"You *stole* Mikael's truck." He chuckled, but quickly sobered. "Did you bring the cash?"

Hadley jerked her head toward the truck. "It's in a backpack inside the cab."

He motioned for her to step away from the vehicle. "A little farther, so the truck doesn't block my view of your hands." Desmond walked sideways to the passenger side of the truck, his eyes and the gun on her at all times.

"Where's my daughter? How do I know she's okay?" Fear gripped Hadley. She needed to know where Sophia was before he discovered she'd only brought a fraction of the ransom he'd demanded. If her daughter were here, on the property, she needed to get to her before Desmond.

"You don't get any information out of me until I see the cash." He reached with one hand and opened the passenger-side door, the gun never wavering.

The backpack sat in the passenger seat. Desmond reached inside, picked it up with one hand, closed the door with his hip and plopped the pack on the sidewall of the truck bed. "Feels light. Let's make sure it's got real money inside and isn't simply full of air." Manic laughter erupted from him as if he thought he were the funniest man alive.

He laid his rifle on the truck roof. "Don't try anything funny. Got it? I promise, I'll be faster than you can be."

Hadley nodded. Hope and fear waged a war inside her. On the one hand, she hoped Mikael would use this moment to confront the man, while his defenses were down. But on the other hand, she feared if Mikael made a sudden move, the man would reach for his weapon and shoot one of them.

"What is this?" Desmond demanded, pulling out a fistful of money. "Why aren't the bills bundled?" He shoved the money into his pants pocket, then reached back in and pulled out some more. This time a pink sock was mixed in with the wadded bills. "I knew it!"

He opened his hand and dropped the loot into the back of the truck. Then he reached inside the backpack once more. This time pulling out a shirt and a pair of jeans along with a couple of hundred dollars. "You're trying to pull a fast one."

"No! I promise I'm not. You didn't give me enough time to come up with the cash." She took a step toward the truck and froze. His right hand hovered over his weapon. "Please," Hadley pleaded with him "That's twenty-seven thousand dollars. It's all the money I have."

Something akin to sympathy flashed across his face, but he narrowed his eyes and it was gone. "Looks like your little girl is going to get a new mommy after all. Too bad. I tried to give you a chance to reunite with your little girl, but I'm a businessman. I have to give the goods to the person who is willing to pay the most."

His words hit her like a tsunami. Hadley had known there was a good chance he wasn't working alone, but she'd never imagined someone had paid him to abduct Sophia. "Wh-who…" Her thoughts were a web of confusion, making it difficult to form a complete sentence.

"Who's going to be Sophia's new mommy?" He lifted the rifle and rounded the bed of the truck, the barrel pointed at her chest. Desmond leered. "Don't guess it'd hurt to tell you, since she promised to give me an extra fifty thousand to kill you. It's—"

A gunshot rang out and a red stain appeared on his chest. Hadley screamed and covered her mouth with her hand, watching the scene before her play out as if in slow motion. As Desmond's rifle fell onto the ground, he stumbled to his knees and turned to look back at the truck. "Mikael."

The older woman stood in the truck bed, the butt of her rifle against her shoulder as she peered down the barrel.

Mikael. Desmond had only said her name after seeing who shot him. He hadn't identified her as Sophia's *new mommy*. Or had he?

TWENTY

Hadley rushed to Desmond, dropped to the ground beside his lifeless body and placed two fingers against the carotid artery in his neck. No pulse. "He's dead."

She turned and glared at Mikael. "Why did you kill him? He didn't tell us where Sophia was. Now we'll never find her."

The older woman laughed and jumped out of the back of the truck. "Did you really think he was going to tell you where she is?" She went over and kicked Desmond's foot, as if to verify for herself that he was truly dead.

"That's what happens to double-crossers. He could have walked away with a hundred grand, if only he hadn't been a greedy buffoon." Mikael turned vacant eyes in her direction. "I didn't really want to get my hands dirty with this part of the job." She shrugged. "But I guess it couldn't be helped. I had to take him out before he realized I was in the truck."

Double-crosser. He could have walked away with a hundred grand. The tiny hairs on the back of Hadley's neck stood at attention. And sweat beaded her hairline, despite the cold December temperatures.

Desmond hadn't said how much the person had promised to pay him for kidnapping Sophia, only that they'd offered him fifty grand for killing Hadley. There was only one way Mikael would know the total amount offered to him. Suddenly cotton-mouthed, she licked her lips, desperate for moisture.

"Ah, I see you finally figured it out." Mikael motioned with her rifle for Hadley to get to her feet. "This worked out for the best anyway. I got to thinking after your boyfriend showed up that just being a blood relative wouldn't be enough to convince the judge to let me raise Sophia. I mean, I don't think Ryan is her daddy, but she has to have one somewhere. Unless he's dead. Is he?"

Hadley stared at the other woman. *Blood relatives*? What? She shook her head, desperate to clear her mind so she could focus on getting out of here alive.

"Drats. I was afraid of that. I guess it was too much to hope for that he was dead," Mikael continued, obviously thinking Hadley's headshake had been an answer. "No matter. I have an idea that will work better and, since her dad hasn't been in the picture, should guarantee Sophia is never taken away from me."

Mikael's words penetrated her consciousness and spurred Hadley into action. She charged toward the older woman, sliding to a stop when Mikael raised the rifle and aimed it at her.

"Don't come any closer." Mikael walked around the truck, her eyes never leaving Hadley. She opened the passenger-side door, removed something from the glove compartment and then kicked the truck door closed.

"Can you please tell me why you're doing this?" Hadley hated the desperate pleading sound in her voice.

"I could." Mikael shrugged. "But what's the point? It's not like you knowing will make a difference. Either way, you're going to die, and I am going to raise Sophia."

Over my dead, cold...oh, wait that's exactly what she's planning. Hadley breathed in a deep breath and slowly released it. Ryan would be looking for her. He probably has the entire ranch out searching.

Unless Carlton is in on this, too. Taking slow, steady breaths, she tamped down the anxiety that threatened to overtake her. Carlton had sincerely seemed worried about Sophia. There was no way he knew what his daughter had done. He would help Ryan find Hadley. She just needed to keep Mikael talking and buy as much time as possible. *Lord, give me the words to say to get Mikael to talk, so I can understand why she is doing this. And please, let her tell me where she's hidden Sophia.*

One-handedly, Mikael shook open a sheet of paper, reached across the hood of the truck and tucked it under the windshield wiper, and then clipped an ink pen to the paper. "Sign the paper."

"What is it?" Hadley reached out with an unsteady hand and tugged the paper free from the wiper.

"Think of it as your last will and testament. It says the sum of your worldly possessions are to go into a trust for Sophia. And you're naming me her guardian."

"Why would anyone believe I'd do that? It's not like we're close friends or anything."

"They'll believe it," Mikael through gritted teeth. "Now sign it."

"No. Not until I get answers." She squared her shoulders and prayed she looked more composed than she felt.

Mikael lifted the gun, propped the butt against her shoulder, leaned her cheek against the stock and looked down the barrel at Hadley, but she stood her ground.

Her only hope for survival was to stall until

Ryan could reach her. No. While she had no doubt Ryan and his trio of friends were searching for her, she couldn't rely on him making it to her in time. After all, Misty Hollow Ranch was a large spread. If Hadley were going to get out of this alive and rescue Sophia, she would have to rely on her own wits.

Lord, please, let this work.

"Okay. Shoot me." Hadley held out her hands, palms upward, and shrugged. "You're not going to let me out of here alive anyway. So do it."

"You think I won't? Is this some kind of game to you?" Mikael glared at her. "Sign. The. Paper."

She shook her head. "No. If the end outcome is me dead, then it doesn't matter if I sign the paper or not. So I choose not to sign it."

"Fine by me." Mikael rounded the front of the truck, the rifle still aimed at Hadley's chest. "I didn't originally plan to have you sign a guardianship paper anyway. I only adjusted the plan after Desmond got greedy. Of course, I shouldn't be surprised by his greed. He went rogue from the very beginning. I'll never understand what he was thinking shooting into your house. He could have killed my Sophia."

My Sophia. Hadley gritted her teeth. She needed Mikael to keep talking. Pointing out Sophia wasn't *hers* wouldn't work well in her favor. "Why did you have him ransack my house?"

"I thought, if you were afraid to be in your home, you'd come to us. With you and Sophia staying on the ranch, I could have arranged an accident to take you out and leave Sophia an orphan." Mikael knelt beside the dead ranch hand's body and picked up his rifle, which lay on the ground beside him.

Regret that she'd missed the opportunity of grabbing his weapon washed over Hadley. She'd been so focused on Mikael and the rifle pointed at her that she'd forgotten about Desmond's weapon.

Pull it together. Sophia is depending on you.

"Sophia needs me. I'm her mother." Hadley shivered at the pure hatred she saw in the other woman's eyes as she advanced closer.

"I'll give her a good life. She'll forget all about you."

Though the sheer thought of Troy's family claiming rights to Sophia terrified Hadley, she knew that threat might be the only information she could leverage to keep Mikael talking. "No. She won't." *Make it sound believable.* "Her father will make sure she remembers me."

"Is that so? Then where's he been for Sophia's entire life?" Mikael scoffed. "That's right, she told me she didn't have a daddy."

Think fast. Keep it close to the truth and make it believable. "He had business out of the country the last few years. But he's back now. That's what Ryan came to tell me. Troy's back. And he and his brother who's a lawyer aren't happy with the situation as it stands now."

"So your baby's daddy is back in the picture? Well, too bad. He's not going to get my little girl." Mikael backhanded Hadley.

Tears stung her eyes and a coppery taste in her mouth made her stomach turn. She gingerly touched her lip and then pulled back her hand to look at the red, sticky blood she knew she'd see. The side of her mouth was already swelling; she'd have a bruise in the morning. If she lived that long.

Planting her feet firmly, she looked the other woman in the eyes. Hazel. The same shade as Carlton's. And Hadley's. Why hadn't she noticed the similarities sooner? And when she looked beneath the generous sprinkling of gray framing Mikael's face, Hadley realized their naturally curly hair was the same shade of blond. *Blood relatives.* "You're my sister."

"No. And I never will bc," the older woman snarled. "Just because my dad fathered you, it doesn't make us sisters. It takes more than blood to be a family."

Hadley pressed her lips together and winced. Mikael's words weren't wrong, but they still stung. Carlton had had four months to tell her she was his daughter. But he hadn't. Didn't matter. Henry Bryant had been her dad, and he'd never treated her as anything less than his pride and joy.

"You're right. I had a wonderful dad, and I'm not looking for a replacement." *Talk to her like you would to an upset student. Defuse the situation.* "I'm sorry if you thought I was here to find my long-lost family or something. Honestly, I had no clue of the connection. Sophia and I can move. You'll never have to see us again."

"Do you think I'll fall for your innocent act? I know you came here to lay claim to the ranch and take my inheritance. You're just like your mom. Take. Take. Take. She took my place as caregiver of my brother after my mom died. Then she killed him."

Hadley blanched. "She wouldn't have—"

"Oh, they said it was SIDS. I don't believe it. C.J. would be alive today if I'd been the one caring for him." She shook her head. "But even so, your mom wanted more than to just be the nanny. I knew it the instant I saw her. She wanted it all. The house. The land. And my dad. It didn't matter that he was a grieving widower. She laid her sights on him from day one." Mikael's eyes narrowed and her nostrils flared. "I don't know why I didn't recognize you the moment I saw you. Minus the eyes and hair color, you look just like her. Should have known one day she'd send you to finish what she started, and claim a share of the ranch."

Disbelief washed over Hadley. Had she heard correctly? For the first time since discovering her second birth certificate, she regretted not confronting her mother and asking about her real father. If she had, she could've avoided this entire situation. "Carlton knew I was out there somewhere and never tried to find me?" She didn't even try to hide the disgust in her voice. "That's some dad you've got there. Turns his back on a young woman and leaves her to raise their child alone."

"Actually, he didn't know about your existence. Unfortunately for your mother, I brought in the mail each day after school. I intercepted the letter she wrote telling my dad about you. It was so easy to silence your mother and keep the truth from him." Manic laughter erupted from her half sister. "I've always regretted I couldn't share my brilliance with anyone, but you're going to die anyway, so it can't hurt to tell you."

A faraway look crossed Mikael's face, and for half a second, Hadley wondered if she could sneak away while the other woman was lost in her memories. No, she'd only get one chance at escape, so she had to be sure the timing was right. "I'd like to hear the story. Tell me how a

child was able to intercept a letter and hide a secret like that."

"I wasn't a child. I was twelve, and very ma-
ture. Which is why I should have been allowed
to take care of C.J. after my mom died." Mikael
looked down the barrel of the rifle. "And you
never would have existed."

The faint sound of horses on the other side of
the ridge they crossed earlier sent hope soaring
inside her. Whether it was Ryan and his crew
or the wild Mustangs she'd seen on her various
trips to the ranch didn't matter. What did matter
was making Mikael think it was a rescue party.
"Ryan!" Hadley exclaimed.

"No!" Mikael cried and looked over her shoulder.

Spurred into action by her captor's momen-
tary distraction, Hadley dashed around the side
of the old miner's shack. And a bullet rang out,
hitting the wall behind her. Forcing herself to
stay focused, Hadley ran with all her might and
didn't look back.

"That was a gunshot!" Ryan pressed his heels
into the quarter horse's side and urged the animal to go faster.

Carlton and Ryan raced down the side of the
mountain to the valley below. Pulling back on
their reins, they slowed their horses to a trot.

"Look," Ryan said, pointing to the hill behind the old miner's shack, "there's Hadley running toward the old mine."

"That area is too rocky. We'll have to hitch our horses to the porch posts and make our way to her."

Ryan scanned the area. "I don't see Mikael. Do you?"

"No." Concern punctuated the older man's one word answer.

They dismounted beside Mikael's truck and walked the horse to the railing.

A man's body lay on the ground, a gunshot through his chest.

"Desmond," Carlton bit out.

"We can't help him now. Stay here. I'll find the girls." Ryan took off around the old shack and stopped at the corner of the building to survey the sight before him.

Hadley was racing up the hill in the direction of the old mine, and Mikael was trudging along behind her with a rifle in her hand. Static sounded in his ear. They had ridden out of range of the others. It was possible the signal would pick back up as he moved around, but he highly doubted it. Besides, as much as he'd like to have communication, especially with his profiler brother-in-law, he knew undistracted concentration was more important at the moment.

So he reached up, removed the earpiece and shoved it into his pocket. Then rested his hand on his holster.

"Look, I'm sure you know how to handle that thing," Carlton stated flatly, coming up behind him. "But let me remind you, I have two daughters. And I don't want *either one of them* shot."

"I don't go into a situation looking to shoot people." He tamped down his annoyance at the man's words. Ryan would never fire his gun at anyone if there were another option. Today would be no different, but he would not hesitate to protect Hadley. He hadn't been there when Jessica needed him most; he would not fail another woman he loved.

Ryan turned and glared at Carlton. "I told you to stay put."

"Too bad. Those are my girls, and this is my land. I'm not staying behind." The older man stood his ground.

"Fine. But keep quiet. We don't want to startle Mikael."

Carlton looked like he might argue, but instead he pressed his lips together. Ryan nodded. "Okay, follow me."

They ran along the bank of the frozen creek, parallel to the hill. Ryan prayed they would intercept Mikael before she reached Hadley. If not, he hoped he'd at least be close enough to take out Mikael if she seemed ready to shoot.

Ryan kept his eyes glued on the woman with the gun. She had to have heard them arrive. Why wasn't she checking to see if they were following her? Shoulders squared and face straight. Eyes zeroed in on her target. She reminded him of a soldier who was laser focused on her mission to take out the enemy. Her demeanor terrified him. The determination etched on her face told him she would not willingly stop until she had accomplished her goal.

But Ryan would stop her. He had to.

Motioning for Carlton to stay behind him, Ryan started up the hill. In spite of having an artificial hip, the older man stayed on his heels, most likely fueled by adrenaline. In no time, they reached the crest and ducked behind a tree to assess the situation.

Hadley reached the old boarded-up mine and turned with a panicked expression on her face. A mountain wall stood behind her. There was no place for her to run. She looked toward the tree where he and Carlton hid. Did she know they were there?

"Maybe Mikael killed Desmond in self-defense and Hadley got scared. That's why she's running." Carlton whispered. "Mikael's chasing after her to protect her."

Ryan frowned at Hadley's father. He suppressed his anger at the wishful expression on

Carlton's face. This was real life, not some drama where you could write your own happy ending. Without saying a word, Ryan turned back to the scene unfolding before him, then he stepped out from behind the tree and froze.

Oblivious to his presence, Mikael walked toward Hadley. Slowly. Purposefully. The rifle cradled in her arms. A smirk on her face. "You look tired, little sister. Running uphill, through the snow, to a dead end must have been exhausting." She guffawed. "Should've gone at a more leisurely pace like me. We both got to the same point, only I'm not even breaking a sweat."

He reached to unholster his weapon, and Carlton put a hand on his arm.

"I'm sure it's a big misunderstanding." The older man's eyes pleaded with him. "Let me talk to her."

Ryan shook his head. "You won't be able to reach her," he whispered, never taking his eyes off the scene before him. "The look on her face is the same as a soldier in combat. Someone who is zoned in on a mission will not hear or see anything else around them." Ryan pulled his Glock from its holster. "They are only focused on killing the enemy."

Hadley caught a glimpse of movement in her peripheral vision. Ryan. He was working his way from tree to tree, getting closer with every step. She took a deep breath.

Time to get Mikael talking about her brilliant scheme. When she was boasting, she seemed to be distracted from her intent to kill Hadley. "You managed to hide my existence for almost twenty-nine years. How exactly did you pull off such a feat?"

"Easy. I learned to forge my dad's writing and signature at an early age. Came in handy for writing excuses for school if I wanted to play hooky. Or, in this case, writing a letter to your mother telling her she wasn't wanted in our lives and demanding she get rid of the *unwanted* child. I even took twenty-five hundred dollars out of Dad's safe and had Desmond purchase a money order, which I included in the letter. So she could get rid of you." Mikael glared at her. "I should have known she wouldn't do as instructed."

The fact that both she and her mother had to make the difficult choice to hide their children to protect them from fathers—or in this case a half sister—who didn't want them wasn't lost on Hadley. Under normal circumstances, she'd seek out a quiet place to reflect and pray. And grieve for what her mother had gone through. But that would have to wait until she found a way out of this situation. *Keep Mikael talking.* "How were you able to convince Desmond to help you do something like that?"

"Easy. He would drink and gamble on his days off, and he lost more than he could afford one Saturday night. I overheard him asking some of the ranch hands for a loan. I told him I'd give him the money to pay off his debt if he helped me. If he didn't, I'd tell Daddy what I'd heard."

Hadley saw Ryan put a restraining hand on Carlton, who was obviously not happy about what he was hearing.

"I see you looking behind me, searching for your boyfriend to come rescue you. Don't think you're going to trick me again into believing he's back there. You tricked me once when you heard the wild Mustangs. Won't happen again." Mikael motioned with her rifle for Hadley to walk toward the boarded-up entry to the old mine.

Hadley took a few sideways steps, her eyes never leaving her half sister. "I still can't believe you stole money from your dad."

"Like you wouldn't have done the same thing to protect your inheritance from a gold digger." She smirked. "It's fitting that you meet your end here. At the mine my sixth-great-grandfather staked claim to in 1860. I guess I should be thankful to Desmond for setting this up. I can dump your body in the mine. I may not even shoot you. Just bury you alive. No one will think to look for you there."

Hadley swallowed the fear that threatened to overtake her and forced her mind to block out the images of a cold, dark mine shaft with creepy-crawly things. Ryan stepped out into the clearing and slowly inched his way closer to Mikael. He motioned for Hadley to keep talking. Desperate to find a place to hide if there was gunfire, she looked around and saw Carlton run to a bigger pine tree, closer to where she and Mikael stood. Then she spotted a boulder, off to her left.

She took a step backward. "Carlton seemed shocked the money for the ransom wasn't in his safe. I guess you took it to pay Desmond to kidnap Sophia and kill me."

Mikael's face turned red and anger radiated off her. "Don't you worry about what I did with that money. It would be rightfully mine one day, anyway. You know what, I'm tired of your jabbering." She lifted the rifle to her shoulder and pointed it at Hadley. "Bye-bye, *little sister*. I'd say it was nice meeting you, but it wasn't."

Hadley dove behind the boulder and the bullet whizzed past her.

"No! Don't!" Carlton yelled. He ran to stand in front of Mikael at the same instant Ryan tackled her from behind. The rifle went off, and a bullet hit Carlton in the thigh. He fell to the ground, a red stain instantly covering the white snow.

Hadley raced to the man who she'd just

learned was her biological father, tears freezing on her eyelashes. Dropping to the ground beside him, she removed the knitted scarf her mother had made for her fourteenth birthday and tied it tightly around the leg to slow the bleeding. "What were you thinking, running in front of a gun?"

"I had to stop one daughter from killing the other… I'm sorry… If I had known about you all those years ago…"

"It's okay. Don't waste your energy on words right now. We'll talk after we get your leg taken care of." She patted his hand and looked over to Ryan, who stood with his gun pointed at Mikael. Hadley's half sister sat with her back against a tree, her face in her hands, crying uncontrollably. At least it seemed the woman felt some remorse for shooting her father.

But there was still unfinished business. Hadley had to find Sophia. She pushed to her feet and made her way over to the woman who had tried to kill her. "Where's my daughter?" she demanded.

Sobs racking her body, Mikael looked up and stared blankly in her direction.

"Where's Sophia?" Hadley took a step toward Mikael. She'd shake the information out of the woman if necessary.

A strong arm wrapped around her waist and

pulled her back until she rested against a hard chest. "We'll get her to talk," Ryan said softly into her ear. "But you won't find out anything with her in this state."

"But—"

"We'll find her. I promise."

Without a doubt, she knew he'd keep that promise.

The sound of snowmobiles reached them seconds before three of the vehicles burst through the trees. Sawyer, Lincoln and Agent Fowler on two of them and one of the ranch hands on the other. The ranch hand rushed to check on Carlton, and Agent Fowler immediately handcuffed Mikael.

"Looks like the cavalry has arrived," Ryan said as Lincoln and Sawyer walked over to them. "We still don't know where Sophia is, so—"

"She's at the house with Bridget." Sawyer turned to Hadley. "Sophia is fine. Bridget and I found her at the hunting cabin. She'd been locked inside. After we managed to get the door open, we found her asleep on a sheepskin rug. We have medics on the way, just so they can check her out. But when I left, she was eating a bowl of oatmeal and talking ninety to nothing to my wife."

Relief surged through her body, replacing the

fear she'd held close since Sophia was abducted. Hadley slumped against Ryan.

He tightened his hold on her and kissed her temple. "Sawyer, go ahead and take Hadley to Sophia. I'll stay here unt—"

"No. I want you to come with me," Hadley interrupted, not even caring there was desperation in her voice. She wanted to hold Sophia in her arms with Ryan by her side.

"I'll be there soon, sweetheart. I promise." He kissed her forehead, and she wrapped her arms around his waist. "Go with Sawyer. When I'm finished here, I'll take you back to Eagle Creek so you can spend Christmas morning in your own home."

A lump formed in her throat. It seemed Ryan couldn't wait to be rid of her. The moments they'd shared while on the run must not have meant as much to him. She stepped out of his arms and forced a smile. "Okay."

Ryan pulled his brother-in-law aside for a quick private conversation, and then Sawyer took her elbow and guided her toward the snowmobile. "Sophia seems to be a resilient child. I don't think you have to worry about her suffering…"

Sawyer rattled on, but Hadley only half listened. She hoped he was right and Sophia wouldn't suffer any long-term effects from the ordeal she'd been put through. However, while her daughter might have the ability to overcome the adversity she'd experienced quickly, Hadley doubted she'd be so blessed. Not only did she have to deal with the trauma from discovering Carlton was her father and her half sister wanted her dead, but also a big piece of her heart would soon be headed back to Colorado.

Almost five hours later, Ryan pulled his SUV into Hadley's freshly shoveled driveway. The neighbor's teenage son must have taken care of it. She'd have to send him a thank-you note along with his usual payment. That was when she noticed the white lights decorating the outside of her home were on and the living room curtains were open, revealing the Christmas tree, which was also lit up and standing tall.

She turned to Ryan. "What...how?"

A smile lifted the corners of his mouth. He put the vehicle into Park and turned to her. "I hope it's okay. I didn't want you and Sophia to come home to a ransacked house."

"But how did you accomplish this?"

He shrugged. "You forget I'm a security specialist. I'm good at picking up clues and filing them away for later use."

She crossed her arms and waited.

"Okay. I'll tell you all my secrets." He chuckled. "I saw the check on the refrigerator made out to Trey Cline. You had written *snow removal* on the *For* line. When I pulled Sawyer aside earlier, I asked him to try and track down Trey since I thought he might be the son of a neighbor and said neighbor might know if you kept a spare key hidden somewhere."

"I don't."

"No. But Trey knew the code to your garage door since he sometimes waters your plants when you and Sophia go on vacation during the summer." He shrugged. "I had a hunch, which Trey confirmed for me, that the local police may have failed to lock the door into the house from the garage when they locked up as we left Thursday."

"So Trey, the seventeen-year-old high school quarterback who lives next door, did all this?" She swept her hand to indicate the house and driveway.

"He shoveled the drive, which he said was *on him*. Although I will give him a Christmas bonus. The rest of it was done by a cleaning crew that I hired."

"On Christmas Eve? That must have cost a fortune."

"It's my gift to you." He took her hands in his. "Please, don't be mad. Normally, I'd never invade—"

She lifted an eyebrow. "You mean break into."

He squirmed and she bit back a smile.

"Well, technically, yes. But I only wanted to expunge as many of the bad memories that I could, so you'd feel safe entering your home again." Ryan glanced in the back seat at her sleeping child, then lowered his voice and added, "I can't erase any of the other things you went through today or the things you'll face over the next few months, but I could do this."

His sincerity and thoughtfulness touched her soul in a way no other person ever had. He was right. No one could take away the emotional turmoil she'd go through as she tried to form a relationship with her biological father or when she testified in court against her half sister. But the thing she dreaded facing most and that would hurt beyond words was Ryan leaving. Her chest tightened. She blinked and turned away, praying he hadn't seen the tears that stung her eyes.

Ryan tucked her hair behind her ear and then used his thumb to wipe away a stray tear. "Hey, what's wrong? I'm sorry if you're upset with me. I shouldn't have—"

"No. I'm not upset. I'm grateful. What you did was very thoughtful. Thank you."

"Then why the tears?"

Hadley bit her lip and shook her head. "Nothing. I'm just being overly emotional. Let me get

Sophia. I'm sure you're anxious to get on the road. It's a long drive to your parents' house."

"Oh." His face fell. "I had hoped I could stay here a few days. Well, not here…at a hotel nearby."

"Why?"

"To see Sophia's face on Christmas morning. To give you both the gifts I bought at the big-box store a few days ago. To spend time with you both without being on the run for our lives."

"But why wouldn't you go home and spend Christmas with your family?" She held her breath. Afraid of the answer but hoping, at the same time, that he'd tell her he loved her and Sophia as much as they loved him. The moment she'd seen Sophia's eyes light up when she saw Ryan for the first time after her abduction, Hadley had known her daughter's heart would be just as broken as hers when he walked out of their lives.

"Don't you know?" He buried his fingers in her hair, his eyes locked on hers. "I'm head over heels for the Logan girls. And while I'm sure there will be a lot of things to work out logistically, I would like permission to court you. In hopes that one day both you and Sophia will change your last name to mine."

Her heart swelled and the tears that had threatened earlier flowed freely now. Only, this time they were tears of joy. "I love you, Ryan Vincent."

"And I love you." He lowered his head and claimed her lips in a tender kiss.

"Mommy." Sophia's sleepy voice sounded from the back seat. "Are we there yet?"

Hadley pulled back and smiled at Ryan. "Yes, baby. We're finally home." And for the first time in six years, she knew she was exactly where she was supposed to be.

EPILOGUE

One year later

Ryan stood next to the large, rock fireplace inside the rustic barn where his and Hadley's guests were gathered for their wedding reception, watching his new bride and daughter talking and laughing with Bridget, who stood with her arms wrapped under her burgeoning belly. After almost losing her life, twice, and then the doctors telling her she might never be able to have a baby, it was hard to imagine that in two months his feisty sister would hold her own daughter in her arms. He had no doubt she and Sawyer would be amazing parents.

"Admiring your new family?" Linc spoke beside him.

"And counting my blessings." He turned to his best friend and almost brother-in-law. "You know, even though I found happiness again, a part of me will always—"

"I know." Linc clapped him on the shoulder. "I also know Jessica would firmly approve of the new Mrs. Ryan Vincent."

"I think so, too."

Across the room, Carlton McIntyre embraced Hadley in a hug and then lifted a giggling Sophia into the air.

"It looks like Hadley and Carlton are growing closer."

He nodded. "They are. She still refers to him as Carlton, but she told Sophia she could call him Grandpa. So it's a start. Hopefully, they'll be able to build a father-daughter relationship now that Mikael's trial is over."

The trial had been postponed a number of times and had only ended three weeks prior to the wedding. Ryan had been so proud of how well Hadley had held up during the trial, especially with all the media coverage that surrounded it.

"I just pray Mikael will eventually allow Carlton to visit her in prison. So far, she has rejected any contact he has tried to have with her." Ryan sighed. "The likelihood of her getting out on parole in his lifetime is slim. Not seeing her is taking a toll on him."

"I'll be praying, too." Linc reached into his pocket and extracted a business envelope and held it out to him. "Looks like your bride is headed your way. Here's the wedding present you asked me to work on."

"You got it? Notarized and legal?"

Linc smiled, turned, kissed Hadley's cheek and patted Sophia on the head. Then he walked away.

"What were you two talking about? I hope it wasn't business," Ryan's beautiful bride said as she wrapped her arms around him. "You promised you wouldn't let anything interfere with our week in Hawaii."

"And I won't." He kissed her soundly on the lips. "This, my dear, is a wedding present from me to you, and Sophia."

Hadley opened the envelope and read the single sheet of paper, her mouth dropping open. "Really? How did you get Troy to agree to sign away his rights?"

"I visited him two weeks ago to tell him why it was a good idea. He said he'd think about it. Apparently, Linc decided to visit him, too, and was able to persuade him to sign the paperwork."

Sophia tapped his leg. "I wanna see the present."

He scooped his daughter into his arms. "What present?"

"The one you gave mommy. You said it was a present for her and me."

Laughing, he kissed his daughter's cheek. "It's

just a piece of paper that says in a few weeks you'll officially be a Vincent."

"But I'm already a Vincent. The minister said so."

"When, honey?" Hadley asked.

"Right after Daddy gave you and me rings." Sophia huffed and held out her hand. The small gold band with the little diamond heart glittered on her right-hand ring finger. "Then you kissed Daddy and the preacher said I present Mr. and Mrs. Ryan Vincent and their daughter Sophia." She pointed to her chest. "That's me. Sophia Ann Logan Vincent."

"Yes, it is, sweetheart." Ryan kissed the top of his darling daughter's head and pulled his wife into a tight embrace. *Thank You, Lord, for placing Hadley and Sophia in my life to teach me that I could have more than one love in my lifetime.*

What was it Grandmother Vincent used to say? *My arms are full, but my heart is fuller.* Amen.

* * * * *

*If you liked this story from Rhonda Starnes,
check out her previous
Love Inspired Suspense books:*

Rocky Mountain Revenge
Perilous Wilderness Escape
Tracked Through the Mountains

Available now from Love Inspired Suspense!

*Find more great reads at
www.LoveInspired.com.*

Dear Reader,

Some seasons of life are more challenging than others, and it's easy to feel like we're carrying the burdens of the world on our shoulders. It was one such season I found myself in while finishing *Abducted at Christmas*. My deadline was looming, and I had to dig deep within myself to focus and get words on the page.

During this time, I felt great empathy for Ryan. The weight of the burdens he carried on his shoulders for six years was so great that his relationship with God was fractured and he closed himself off to love. Once he remembered Who was in control, Ryan's load didn't seem as heavy, and his heart opened to love again. A reminder we all need once in a while.

I would love to hear from you. Please connect via my website www.rhondastarnes.com or email contact@rhondastarnes.com.

All my best,
Rhonda Starnes

Get 3 FREE REWARDS!

We'll send you 2 FREE Books plus a FREE Mystery Gift.

Both the **Love Inspired®** and **Love Inspired®** Suspense series feature compelling novels filled with inspirational romance, faith, forgiveness and hope.

YES! Please send me 2 FREE novels from the Love Inspired or Love Inspired Suspense series and my FREE gift (gift is worth about $10 retail). After receiving them, if I don't wish to receive any more books, I can return the shipping statement marked "cancel." If I don't cancel, I will receive 6 brand-new Love Inspired Larger-Print books or Love Inspired Suspense Larger-Print books every month and be billed just $6.49 each in the U.S. or $6.74 each in Canada. That is a savings of at least 16% off the cover price. It's quite a bargain! Shipping and handling is just 50¢ per book in the U.S. and $1.25 per book in Canada.* I understand that accepting the 2 free books and gift places me under no obligation to buy anything. I can always return a shipment and cancel at any time by calling the number below. The free books and gift are mine to keep no matter what I decide.

Choose one: ☐ **Love Inspired Larger-Print**
(122/322 BPA GRPA)

☐ **Love Inspired Suspense Larger-Print**
(107/307 BPA GRPA)

☐ **Or Try Both!**
(122/322 & 107/307 BPA GRRP)

Name (please print)

Address   Apt. #

City   State/Province   Zip/Postal Code

Email: Please check this box ☐ if you would like to receive newsletters and promotional emails from Harlequin Enterprises ULC and its affiliates. You can unsubscribe anytime.

Mail to the Harlequin Reader Service:
IN U.S.A.: P.O. Box 1341, Buffalo, NY 14240-8531
IN CANADA: P.O. Box 603, Fort Erie, Ontario L2A 5X3

Want to try 2 free books from another series? Call 1-800-873-8635 or visit www.ReaderService.com.

*Terms and prices subject to change without notice. Prices do not include sales taxes, which will be charged (if applicable) based on your state or country of residence. Canadian residents will be charged applicable taxes. Offer not valid in Quebec. This offer is limited to one order per household. Books received may not be as shown. Not valid for current subscribers to the Love Inspired or Love Inspired Suspense series. All orders subject to approval. Credit or debit balances in a customer's account(s) may be offset by any other outstanding balance owed by or to the customer. Please allow 4 to 6 weeks for delivery. Offer available while quantities last.

Your Privacy—Your information is being collected by Harlequin Enterprises ULC, operating as Harlequin Reader Service. For a complete summary of the information we collect, how we use this information and to whom it is disclosed, please visit our privacy notice located at corporate.harlequin.com/privacy-notice. From time to time we may also exchange your personal information with reputable third parties. If you wish to opt out of this sharing of your personal information, please visit readerservice.com/consumerschoice or call 1-800-873-8635. **Notice to California Residents**—Under California law, you have specific rights to control and access your data. For more information on these rights and how to exercise them, visit corporate.harlequin.com/california-privacy.

LIRLIS23

Get 3 FREE REWARDS!

We'll send you 2 FREE Books plus a FREE Mystery Gift.

FREE
Value Over
$20

Both the **Harlequin® Special Edition** and **Harlequin® Heartwarming™** series feature compelling novels filled with stories of love and strength where the bonds of friendship, family and community unite.

YES! Please send me 2 FREE novels from the Harlequin Special Edition or Harlequin Heartwarming series and my FREE Gift (gift is worth about $10 retail). After receiving them, if I don't wish to receive any more books, I can return the shipping statement marked "cancel." If I don't cancel, I will receive 6 brand-new Harlequin Special Edition books every month and be billed just $5.49 each in the U.S. or $6.24 each in Canada, a savings of at least 12% off the cover price, or 4 brand-new Harlequin Heartwarming Larger-Print books every month and be billed just $6.24 each in the U.S. or $6.74 each in Canada, a savings of at least 19% off the cover price. It's quite a bargain! Shipping and handling is just 50¢ per book in the U.S. and $1.25 per book in Canada.* I understand that accepting the 2 free books and gift places me under no obligation to buy anything. I can always return a shipment and cancel at any time by calling the number below. The free books and gift are mine to keep no matter what I decide.

Choose one: ☐ **Harlequin**   ☐ **Harlequin**   ☐ **Or Try Both!**
                  Special Edition   **Heartwarming**   (235/335 & 161/361
                  (235/335 BPA GRMK)   **Larger-Print**   BPA GRPZ)
                                           (161/361 BPA GRMK)

Name (please print)

Address   Apt. #

City   State/Province   Zip/Postal Code

Email: Please check this box ☐ if you would like to receive newsletters and promotional emails from Harlequin Enterprises ULC and its affiliates. You can unsubscribe anytime.

Mail to the **Harlequin Reader Service:**
IN U.S.A.: P.O. Box 1341, Buffalo, NY 14240-8531
IN CANADA: P.O. Box 603, Fort Erie, Ontario L2A 5X3

Want to try 2 free books from another series! Call 1-800-873-8635 or visit www.ReaderService.com.

---

*Terms and prices subject to change without notice. Prices do not include sales taxes, which will be charged (if applicable) based on your state or country of residence. Canadian residents will be charged applicable taxes. Offer not valid in Quebec. This offer is limited to one order per household. Books received may not be as shown. Not valid for current subscribers to the Harlequin Special Edition or Harlequin Heartwarming series. All orders subject to approval. Credit or debit balances in a customer's account(s) may be offset by any other outstanding balance owed by or to the customer. Please allow 4 to 6 weeks for delivery. Offer available while quantities last.

Your Privacy—Your information is being collected by Harlequin Enterprises ULC, operating as Harlequin Reader Service. For a complete summary of the information we collect, how we use this information and to whom it is disclosed, please visit our privacy notice located at corporate.harlequin.com/privacy-notice. From time to time we may also exchange your personal information with reputable third parties. If you wish to opt out of this sharing of your personal information, please visit readerservice.com/consumerschoice or call 1-800-873-8635. **Notice to California Residents**—Under California law, you have specific rights to control and access your data. For more information on these rights and how to exercise them, visit corporate.harlequin.com/california-privacy.

HSEHW23